ABOUT THE AUTH

Mike Williamson has spent most of his life in and around aircraft, but has always wanted to write a novel, unfortunately, life in the way of earning a living and bringing up children got in the way. Having taken an early retirement, he now has the time to devote to his wishes, and he has chosen science fiction as the genre, but look out in the future for other stories.

Science fiction is probably the most flexible genre possible, as all of the others can be included, so for example you can have sf crime, sf romance, or pure sf, etc. With Mike's technical background he obtains inspiration from small items of information in science and engineering. This makes his stories more plausible, and he hopes that the reader will enjoy every one of them, and think about today's world – and the future!

For Ernie.

THE

GENESIS

BUG

Mike Williamson

Mike Williamson

DEDICATION

For Lucy

For her forebearance

THE GENESIS BUG

The sleep of reason produces monsters.

Goya: *Los Caprichos.*

Prologue

As the long night shadows closed in, the distant stars appeared one by one, bright, silent witnesses to the fate of the Universe. Below in the realm of mortals, men slept and huddled into their sleeping bags, passing comments and telling stories. Conversations finally became less and eyes closed as the fire's flames became embers.

Above the sleeper's heads, a shooting star appeared; a messenger from the Gods. It split into several parts and rapidly turned to dust, slowing down to drift like gossamer on the winds to settle on the darkened ground and foliage without a sound.

While the slumberers dreamed, a minute speck of that dust unravelled to produce a thin, microscopic hair-like creature, finer than a human hair. It sensed the air and headed for the nearest food source. As it cautiously climbed over a hand that lay carelessly on the ground and weaved around what were to it the giant obstacles of human hair, the sleeper grunted at the tickling, his hand brushing over the small creature that flattened itself against the skin.

When all was still again, the creature wriggled forward and arrived at a prominent vein. It squirted a small amount of anaesthetic liquid on to the skin, and after a few seconds, it inserted its chisel head under the skin without being felt and cut its way towards a nerve. It paused until the blood clotted and sealed the wound, and then continued its journey.

As it moved, it fed on the host's tissue and grew fat. At a certain stage, it stopped and grew longer; the extra length broke away, and both parts continued in different directions, following the network of nerves. As it moved, it divided into an increasing number of parts until it became almost invisible and indistinguishable from its surroundings.

The constellation of Queen Cassiopeia continued to circle Polaris the North Star until the Sun's light dimmed the brightest of stars.

Chapter One

Billy woke suddenly and blinked. He felt like hell! The others were also stirring in their sleeping bags, uttering a few moans and grunts. The dew had settled in his sandy coloured hair and the sky was bright, so bright that it hurt his eyes. He had been sleeping on his right arm, and as the circulation flooded back into the veins, it ached and suffered pins and needles. He gritted his teeth and flexed his fingers. He noticed that the tent had collapsed on them during the night, which explained the view of the open sky beyond the towering redwoods and the dew in his hair.

"Who's making breakfast?" Joel rubbed his face and glared around at the other five school friends. Joel was Billy's gigantic cousin.

"I'll make the coffee," Billy's next door neighbour Sean volunteered from under a lump in the tent's fabric.

"Sean's the man!" exclaimed Joel without too much enthusiasm.

Billy eyed the small mountain of beer cans and realised why his stomach lurched at the thought of breakfast, "I think that I just want coffee after I have a whiz."

He struggled to get out of the sleeping bag and from under the collapsed tent. "Oh God, do I ache. I promise not to drink again and sleep rough in the woods, ever," he promised himself as he wobbled towards some bushes that looked to be miles away.

When he returned, he found that the general consensus was coffee only. He looked at them and thought that he had never seen them in such a bad shape. The school was out, and this was the summer's first adventure. They gulped down Sean's scalding coffee like desperate men.

"I suggest that we sit this one out," Marcus, probably the smartest one there said. He was also the smallest and weakest.

"When the guy in my head with the jackhammer stops, I'll sit up," Gerry lay on his back with his eyes closed.

"We've got all summer to get to the lake," Sean rubbed the sleep from his eyes. He was referring to Crater Lake, Oregon. That's where they were - almost, Oregon, the Timber State. Six refugees from White Tail Butte High School on a little R 'n R, an annual event.

"I've got to get back on Monday, or my ole man'll give me hell!" Joel muttered from behind the arm that he was using to cover his eyes, "Someone turn the light out!"

Gerry started scratching his arms furiously, "I think I've picked up some ticks."

"You probably got them from Sean," Billy joked.

"Ah, the simple pleasures of living in the wild," Marcus gave a chuckle, "I'm itching too. Is there any poison ivy or oak round here?"

"I bloody hope not!" Billy sat up too quickly and winced, "I've just exposed the best part of my body to nature!"

They broke out in a gentle laughter, and Marcus increased their hilarity, "I don't think that's the reason for the swelling!"

Billy realised that the itching that he had felt on waking had got worse. One by one, they all agreed that they had picked up something or walked into a patch of poison oak. Marcus disagreed, "If it was poison oak we would all have violent patches, but all I can see is where we have been scratching."

"Perhaps it was in the beer," Gerry suggested. It was generally agreed that he was the comic of the party.

"The only thing the beer gave us was headaches!" Joel futilely pulled at the tent, "Perhaps we should have put the tent up before opening the cans."

"Remarkable how accurate hindsight can be!" Marcus observed with a chuckle and then a moan.

Billy laughed and winced at the pain it caused, "None of us are in a fit state to drive. I propose that we move on later today or in the morning. At least we can say we saw the lake."

"Much later!" Sean clutched his head.

Chapter Two

The SUV locked all wheels and skidded to a halt, sending the occupants flying and leaving long black marks on the road, and a strong smell of burnt rubber in the air.

"What the hell are you doing Joel?" they chorused from a tangle of arms and legs.

They were at the crossroads on the outskirts of White Tail Butte and Joel sat looking in all directions with a puzzled look on his face. It was a typical country town, dusty and windblown roads, and the industrial buildings tended to look plain but efficient. The original part of the town, the residential part consisted of wooden houses dominated by the spire of All Saint's Church.

"What's the matter Einstein, forget where you live?" Sean pulled himself out of the ruck of arms and legs.

"Just for a moment, I didn't recognise this place at all," with a shake of his head Joel gunned the engine and turned left and headed towards town.

"You've only lived here for all your life," Billy shook his head at his cousin's antics.

"I think the beer melted your brain," Sean leant forward and ruffled Joel's hair.

Joel knocked Sean's hand away and scowled, "It's not funny man; it felt really weird!" They remained quiet as this behaviour was not characteristic of Joel.

One by one Joel dropped off the friends at their addresses, without making an error or needing further directions. Eventually, he pulled into the drive next to his own pickup, stowed the camping equipment in the garage and entered the kitchen. The SUV was his father's that he had borrowed for the trip.

"Have a good trip?" His father was reading a newspaper while enjoying a Sunday beer.

"Yeah, we had a good time, but I feel dead tired. I think I'll lie down for a while." Joel rubbed his eyes.

"You probably got too much sun. I keep telling you to get a proper hat!" his father mildly scolded.

"Shall I make you some food?" his mother called out from the kitchen.

Joel's stomach heaved at the thought, "No thanks, Ma; I'm not that hungry."

Joel lay down on his bed and felt nauseous. He scratched his forearms and looked at them. They looked normal, but the itching was getting worse. As the world spun around him, he closed his eyes and tried to will the feeling away.

In the morning Joel said that he felt better, although he still looked off colour and just pecked at his food. He went with his father to their hardware store to start his summertime job. One day it was expected that he would take over Thomas Hardware.

About mid-morning Gerry made an appearance. He looked as bad as Joel and said that he felt it. Mr Thomas asked if he would like to help out; summer was the time that a lot of households did repairs and improvements, and the stock needed checking.

"Sure Mr Thomas. Shall I check out the screws 'n stuff?"

"That'll be fine. Joel can make out the orders."

About a half hour later, Mr Thomas was just passing Gerry when he stopped in his tracks. Gerry often helped out in the store, and Mr Thomas thought that he was a good worker even if he did clown around, but not this morning. "What are you doing?" he asked.

Gerry turned and looked at him with a blank stare.

"Just look at what you've done," Mr Thomas pointed at the rack of screws.

Gerry looked at the empty box in his hand and then at the bin. He had just put steel and brass screws in the same bin.

"Gee Mr Thomas, I don't know how that happened."

"Well, you had better check out what you've done this morning and put it right," Mr Thomas frowned. Both boys were acting stupid, and he wondered about the others that were on the trip. Were they taking dope?

He didn't have to wait too long for an answer. Billy walked in to see if Joel wanted lunch in the diner.

"Morning Uncle! A great day isn't it?" Billy was bright and cheerful, and Mr Thomas was relieved about the dope question. At least Billy didn't look as spaced out as the other two.

"Morning Billy! Go round the back. I think he's in the office. Gerry's here as well."

He found Joel sitting on a crate with his head in his hands. "What's up?"

Joel looked up, and Billy was surprised to see that his face was grey.

"Hi, Billy, how'd you feel?" Joel groaned.

"Great man, but you look as though you were dying of something."

"Thanks, I was hoping you'd say something encouraging. I've got a buzzing in my ears, and I can't seem to concentrate." Joel poked a finger in each ear and waggled them.

"Do you want to go to the diner?" Billy asked.

"I guess I should; might feel better. Gerry's here somewhere. I heard Dad dressing him down about something."

Gerry declined the offer of lunch, preferring to finish the task. They left him staring blankly at the screws and went to the Barbwire Grill.

"What can I get you guys?" Megan Hughes was in the year after them and had the reputation as a flirt. She was a pretty girl with a blonde ponytail, freckles and brilliant blue eyes. Billy responded to her bright smile although she was looking at Joel.

"I didn't know that you were working here," Billy said.

"Girl's gotta do what a girl's gotta do!" Seeing that Joel wasn't interested, she turned her full attention on to Billy, "There's a dance on Saturday at the Hall. Will you be there?"

"Sure I will. Who else is going?"

"Just about everyone. We should have a great time. I've got a new outfit that'll blow your mind!"

"Then I'll definitely be there!" Billy grinned at her and wondered why he was the centre of her attention. "In the meantime, I'm going to have some of that pizza, coffee and I'll take some blueberry crumble. What do you want Joel?"

Joel pulled his head out of his hands, "Sounds okay to me. I'll have the same."

Megan looked at Joel with a critical eye, "You've got one hell of a hangover! What were you guys doing over the weekend, as though I didn't know? I'll get you a double espresso!"

When the coffee arrived, Joel reached for the sugar.

"I thought that you didn't like sugar in coffee," Billy looked at Joel in surprise.

Joel hesitated, "I feel like it," and then ladled in seven spoonfuls. When he tasted it, he pulled a face and put in two more.

"Do you like coffee with your sugar?" Billy smiled at his cousin's strange behaviour.

Joel played with his food before pushing away the pizza and attacking the blueberry crumble with enthusiasm.

"You seem to be on a sugar jag," Billy observed.

"I'm beginning to feel better already. Can I have your blueberry?" Joel scattered crumbs as he shovelled down large spoonfuls. Billy ordered two more blueberry crumbles and Joel disposed of one quickly.

"I must say, you do look a lot like yourself now," Billy had rescued the other piece of pie for himself before Joel had seen it.

Joel sighed, "I feel much better. All I needed was some sugar; must have burned up too much energy at the weekend."

"We didn't do very much," Billy reminded him.

Joel brushed that aside, "Whatever! I obviously lost some energy, and it needed replacing."

"If it continues, I would see the doctor. You could have a diabetes problem," Billy looked seriously at his cousin. He had never seen him act this way before.

Chapter Three

A stream of cars and pickups were converging on the Old Hall. It was originally the town meeting place but was now given over to social activities when the town had built new municipal offices out of brick for its elected mayor.

No alcohol was allowed; the refreshments were provided in the bar only consisted of root beer and fruit juice, but some of the boys frequently brought hip flasks to make the drinks more interesting.

The band for the evening were the 'Crater Critters' from the school and were surprisingly not bad. As usual, the girls congregated in a protective herd, eyeing the boys and making comments and giggles. The boys were spread out in several groups, trying unsuccessfully not to notice the girls.

"Are you going to give me that dance you promised?" True to form as a flirt, Megan had left the protective huddle of her friends and marched over to Billy, so they were the first on the dance floor, but others soon joined them.

Megan's outfit was very revealing. Billy looked down her cleavage, following the freckles as far as he could, "I like your dress."

Megan could see where he was looking and her eyes sparkled with mischief, "I made it just for you. I just hope that the stitching doesn't come undone."

"We'll have to see what happens later." Billy smiled lewdly.

"In your dreams!" she replied, but her eyes held a promise.

"I'm getting thirsty. Shall I get you something?" Billy asked.

"Oh, kind sir, please get me a blackcurrant with ice," Megan giggled.

"Okay, one icy blackcurrant coming up," Billy pushed his way up to the bar. Sean and Gerry were there.

"I see Megan has lassoed you," Sean dug his elbow into Billy's side.

"I'm just irresistible!" Billy ordered the drinks.

"Guess we won't see you later," Gerry chuckled.

"Where are the other guys?" Billy looked round and ignored their banter.

"I think Joel is still working," Sean pulled a face, "He made a complete hash of the store and he's still sorting it out."

"How did he do that?" Billy knew that Joel was a reliable worker although not a genius.

Gerry shook his head, "I don't know about Joel, but while I was there, everything looked different, and I couldn't concentrate. I think I was still hung-over!"

Sean looked serious, "I think it must have been in the beer, and I'm not going to do that again, at least for a long while."

"Why are you carrying that hip flask then?" Gerry tapped Sean's pocket.

"It's not beer; it's something I cooked up in the cellar!" Sean said defensively.

Billy smiled and brushed them aside. Taking the two drinks, he found Megan surrounded by an eager bunch of hopeful young men. A few hung on until it was obvious that Megan had made her choice, and Billy was giving them a hard stare, and as a star football player, he wasn't to be trifled with.

"You're not safe to be left alone," Billy handed Megan the drink.

Megan giggled, "I guess they have the wrong impression of me."

"I hope not!" and he winced as Megan playfully dug him in the ribs.

They had one more dance and then stood to one side talking to some of their friends.

"I would love another drink," Megan said, "I'm just off to the girl's room while you do that."

Billy made his way to the bar and took two drinks, and made his way back to where they had been standing. Megan was still in the powder room, so he sipped at his glass and looked around. There seemed to be some problem in one corner; raised voices from a small group of guys. He guessed that someone had a bit too much of the modified fruit juice or someone's hormones were over reacting.

Megan turned up at his elbow and took her drink, "There's some problem over a missing girl; they were talking about it in the Girl's Room."

Billy nodded towards the noisy corner, "Anything to do with that?"

"Probably, do you know Suzy Barr?" she looked at Billy who shook his head. "She's a bit of a tramp, or so they say, and really too young to be here."

"You're calling someone else a tramp?" Billy's eyes crinkled up with laughter.

Megan slapped his shoulder, "How long have you known me? I show off, but that's as far as it goes!"

"Unfortunately, I know that is all too true," Billy gave a mock sigh.

"Let's forget them and have another dance," and she dragged him unprotesting on to the dance floor.

Chapter Four

Billy heard the telephone ring as he was dressing in the morning. His mother handed him the phone as he walked into the kitchen, "It's Megan."

Surprised, he took the receiver, "Hi and good morning. Did I forget something, or couldn't you stay away?"

"Hi Billy, thanks for last night, it was great fun. Do you remember that hullabaloo about Suzy?" Her voice had a metallic ring.

"Yeah, what about it?"

"She's gone missing, big time! No one saw her after the dance, and she never made it home."

"Wow! That sounds bad. Who was she with?" Billy came wide awake.

"No one in particular, or more than one and that's bad in itself. The sheriff is making up a search team, and I wondered if you would join them." Megan sounded worried.

"Yeah, sure, I'll ring the guys and tell them. Where are they starting from?"

"The sheriff is calling everyone to the Old Hall. Will you pick me up on the way?" Confirming that, Billy replaced the telephone and started to put on his boots.

"I'm coming too," Billy's father had overheard the conversation. "Do you know the girl?"

Billy shook his head, "By sight maybe, but the name means nothing." He made some calls and found out unsurprisingly that Joel was still asleep and not well. As his father made some further calls, he made his way next door to tell Sean but met him halfway.

"This is bloody awful!" Sean said, "Do we know the girl?"

"Nah, she's a few years younger than us, or so Megan says. Are you coming with us?"

"Dad's getting the drive out now, so I'll go with him." Sean turned away.

A fleet of truck, cars and pickups converged on the Old Hall. There were more vehicles than there was at the dance the night before.

Sheriff Dave Reynolds organised them in groups to search different directions. Billy, his father and Megan were sent towards the forest area while others searched the roads and tracks, and soon the woods echoed with calls and whistles. A small group, including Suzy's mother, stayed with the vehicles.

It was well after lunch before Suzy was found. Megan poked a stick under a bush, and there was a small cry, and then the bush moved violently. Billy and his father walked towards the bush as Megan pushed the branches away. The girl was wearing just her panties, and her skin and hair were covered in dirt and leaves, her eyes wide with fear.

As Megan leant towards her, the girl shrank away from the proffered hand. Megan noticed that her eyes were almost bulging out of their sockets, and there was a dribble of saliva at the corner of the girl's mouth.

"Come on Suzy; it's me Megan." She spoke softly as she would to a lost puppy, "You know me, and there's nothing to be afraid of."

Billy's father slipped off his jacket and handed it to Megan. "Put this on her."

With some difficulty, they got Suzy to stand up and covered her trembling body. "Okay everyone, we've found her alive!" Billy's father yelled out.

There were a series of calls that echoed through the trees and everyone turned round and headed back to the Old Hall. Billy and Megan made slow progress as Suzy could just about walk until Billy picked up the girl and held her tightly.

When they emerged from the trees, the sheriff and Suzy's parents rushed over.

"Well done lad! Where did you find her?" the sheriff asked.

"Under a bush," Billy looked up at the officer as he gently set Suzy down inside a truck, "She was whimpering all the time. Someone or something has scared her real bad."

"She's going to the hospital, and they'll look after her. Can you show me where you found her?" The sheriff hoisted his gunbelt.

"We all can." Billy's father looked pale. Megan joined them as they went back to the bush, and a deputy drove Suzy and her folks away to the hospital.

Chapter Five

Jeremiah Crooke MD ran the small hospital, hardly more than a clinic in White Tail Butte, and usually did little more than set a broken bone or administer medicine and deliver babies. This day was different, and it sent his mind back to his wartime experiences and shell-shocked soldiers. Suzy reminded him of one of those.

She lay curled up on the bed, her eyes wide open in fright, and she gave almost inaudible whimpers. Her mother was trying to comfort her but with little success, while her father stood with a hopeless expression on his face and a hint of anger. The staff of nurses had given her a preliminary check for obvious damage, but apart from the filth and a few thorn scratches, there was nothing obvious. What was needed was a thorough examination, but until the girl had composed herself, it was out of the question.

Crooke gave her a sedative, and she never showed any reaction to the needle. "When she comes round she may feel better." He took Suzy's mother by the arm and guided her and Mister Barr to the door. "Go and have a rest, get some coffee and if you want you can sit with her later."

While Suzy slept, she would be minutely examined for injuries and evidence of sexual activity; a blood sample was taken, and then finally she would be cleaned. If nothing else, she would look better after their ministrations.

He saw Suzy's parents leave for the café and turned to the nurse. "I'm worried about her lack of response.

We should get a psychiatrist in early tomorrow; will you see who's available?" Then he noticed Sheriff Reynolds sitting quietly in the corner.

"You're waiting for some report?" He sat next to the sheriff.

"Yup, do you have any idea what sort of attack this was?" Dave Reynolds looked grim. He'd served his time in Seattle, and didn't expect anything in this sleepy town that he had experienced there.

"At this stage, we're not sure it was an attack. She's in a state of severe shock, and until attended to we have no real idea of anything. In a short while we'll give her a detailed examination which will provide some information, but in the meantime, I'd advise you to go home and come back tomorrow; by then she should be able to give you an explanation as to what happened."

After the sheriff had left, Crooke stood and thought about Suzy. What he had said that it might not have been an attack was worrying. She could have had too much to drink (He was well aware that the boys spiked the juice with spirit.) and there was an alternative that she had some form of nervous breakdown, and that was really worrying. Of course, it could be a boy's amorous attentions had got out of hand, but girls usually threw a tantrum and got over it quickly. He had never seen anyone becoming almost comatose or detached before.

Chapter Six

Megan roused Billy with a 'phone call early the following morning.

"I'd like to see how Suzy is. Would you run me over to the hospital?"

"Yeah, give me some time to get ready, and I'll pick you up." Billy yawned, "I need some coffee first."

"Pick up my jacket while you're there," Billy's father said.

They were kept waiting when they arrived, and eventually Crooke appeared and took them aside.

"She's woken up and none the worse for wear. She has no memory of what has happened, in fact, she was surprised to find herself in the hospital," Crooke gave a tight smile.

"No memory at all?" Megan looked puzzled.

Crooke shook his head, "She remembers dancing, and then nothing until she woke up here. As far as she knows, she didn't take any alcohol or strange substances, and her tests back that up. There wasn't any sexual attack either. You were there, and we're hoping that you could shed some light on the evening."

"I know her by sight, but she's a few years behind us, I didn't even know her name," Billy tried to remember details of that evening.

"The first we knew of any trouble was when I went to the girl's room, and there was a rumour about a girl that had gone missing, and when I came out, there was some trouble with some guys arguing about who she had gone with," Megan filled in.

"Yeah, there was a bit of a fight going on," Billy remembered, "but that's not unusual."

"No one saw her leave with anyone, or even just by herself?" Crooke asked.

Megan shook her head, "We didn't, but maybe someone else did."

"The sheriff is going to question everyone so expect a visit," Crooke said absently, "If you want to see her go ahead, but take it easy."

Suzy looked surprised to see them. She was not part of their circle, but she had spoken to Megan a few times, and she knew of Billy from his exploits on the football team.

"What are you guys doing here?" she asked with a bright smile.

"We were the ones that found you, and we're wondering how you were now," Megan explained.

Suzy pulled a face, "Thanks, I'm okay, but I don't know what happened. I caused everyone a lot of trouble, and I do want to thank you for finding me."

"You were in a hell of a state with hardly any clothes on," Billy gave a little almost apologetic smile; after all, she had a good figure for someone so young.

"Oh yeah, the sheriff was here and asked about that. He's found my stuff scattered around, but I still don't know what happened," Suzy didn't look put out at being found almost naked.

"What was the very last thing you remember?" Megan sat down on the bed, "Did some guy try something?

"No, I wasn't with anyone in particular, but I remember feeling hot, very hot!" Suzy said with conviction.

"When was that?" Billy asked.

"I was with Greg Thomson; I think he's cute! But then I started feeling very hot and uncomfortable, and then I went outside for a cigarette and cool down. Then things got a bit hazy, I remember walking towards the exit and feeling a bit weird, then all I can remember is feeling hot."

"It wasn't that warm," Megan remembered that she had goose bumps when they left the dance, "Could you have taken something, someone slipped you a mickey?"

Suzy shook her head firmly, "I only had one drink, and I got that myself."

"You look alright now," Billy said.

"With my clothes on you mean," Suzy gave him a sly grin.

"You certainly looked alright then," Billy returned the grin.

"Have you had anything happen like this before?" Megan ignored their banter.

"The doc and sheriff have asked the same questions, and I said the same to them; I have no idea of what happened."

"Well, you get better soon," Billy said.

"I feel fine right now, and they said I could go home this afternoon. Thanks for coming!"

"She seems normal to me," Billy said as they walked down the corridor.

"Yeah, but something weird happened," Megan saw Crooke and steered Billy in that direction.

The doctor looked up from his notebook, "What did you think of her?"

"There doesn't appear to be anything wrong now," Megan paused, "but something did happen on the night. She said that she felt hot; is there anything that could have caused that? I thought that if she felt hot, she would have walked into the woods and taken her clothes off to cool down."

Crooke ruminated for a moment before replying, "If we accept that her body temperature rose to an alarming degree, and that would cause disorientation and some bizarre behaviour, and even a loss of memory. As to what caused it, there could be a number of causes."

"You checked her out and said that you couldn't find any sign of drugs," Billy put forward, "but I thought that some drugs can disappear very quickly."

"That's true, and still a possibility, but I favour that something metabolic happened, perhaps a temporary blood clot." Crooke pulled at his lower lip.

"But she was terrified when we found her, I still think that something scared her half to death," Billy said firmly, "you didn't see her face at that time."

"She could have hallucinated as a result of a blood clot," Crooke smiled at their concern, "we all have fears, and when something affects the brain, anything can happen."

Billy didn't look satisfied as they left, "I still think that something frightened her!"

"No, Doc could be right. What could frighten her to take her clothes off and hide under a bush?" Megan folded her arms, "the two things don't go together. Taking your clothes off makes you feel more vulnerable."

Billy thought that over, "Yeah, could be! If something attacked her, then why didn't it finish the job?"

"You forgot your dad's jacket. I'll get it," Megan turned and ran back through the doors.

Chapter Seven

Michael Donovan shuffled through the papers on his desk, and then sat back to think. There was a time when he was an 'ace' reporter during the Yugoslavian conflict, but that changed his ambitions. Many times his life had been in danger, and he had reported as honestly as he could about the atrocities that he had witnessed, but his reports had been heavily censored or completely cancelled. He had decided to seek a quieter and more fulfilling life in a provincial newspaper, and now ran the 'White Tail Butte's News', if it could be called news.

This story before him was hardly better than that of 'a missing cat now found', about a precocious girl who had disappeared at a dance, and then was found safe and well, but unclothed in the forest. It must have happened every weekend somewhere in the state; a 'romantic' meeting gone sour.

What made it worse for him was that nearly the whole town had been involved in the search for her and would know as much as he did, if not more. Not news at all!

It needed some filling he decided, and grabbed his hat and walked down two blocks to the sheriff's office.

"Oh yeah, we were in a panic, but there's not much more to report," Sheriff Reynolds gave the expected and disappointing verdict.

"What about her clothes, did you find them?" Donovan tried to search for something extra.

"Yeah, they were found and returned to her parents." The sheriff didn't appear interested, "they were scattered through the bushes."

"Were they torn, blood-stained?"

"No, they were carefully undone and thrown on the ground," the sheriff snorted, "I reckon one of her boyfriends was involved and something went wrong. These young girls have a habit of starting something they don't want to finish!"

"Who found her?"

"Ahh, Megan Hughes and her boyfriend, Billy Anderson. They were at the dance."

"Who was the girl's boyfriend?" Donovan scribbled the names in his notebook.

The sheriff laughed, "Take your pick; several boys claimed to be, and there was a fight at the dance with one accusing the other when she disappeared."

"She was taken to the hospital; Doc Crooke looked at her?"

"Yeah, but you're wasting your time on this Donovan, it was just a randy couple of kids where things got out of hand," the sheriff dismissed the subject and Donovan with a wave of his hand.

Despite the sheriff's opinion Donovan continued walking towards the hospital but saw Crooke in the Barbwire Grill sipping coffee. He slid into the seat next to him and ordered a coffee.

"You look a picture of health, so you must want me for something else other than an aspirin," Crooke surmised.

"Yeah you guessed right. This young girl Suzy Barr that disappeared at the dance last weekend," Donovan dumped some sugar in his coffee, "any details?"

"I thought that would be it. I can't give specific details, but I can tell you that she didn't ingest GHB or Rohypnol or alcohol, and she wasn't raped. My guess is that she suffered a temporary loss of faculties due to some irregularity in her blood or nervous system."

"That sounds a bit vague," Donovan scribbled in his notebook, "the sheriff thinks that it was a date gone wrong."

"I know he does, but the girl didn't suffer anything more than getting cold and a few scratches."

"Scratches?" Donovan looked up.

"From thorn bushes, I think that she ran wildly and blundered into bushes," Crooke sighed and put down his cup, "there is no evidence of an attack, and that's why I'm keeping an eye on her. She'll come in for weekly checks for a while."

Donovan flicked back through his notebook, "She was found by some school friends. What do you know about them?"

"Ask them yourself; that's Megan there who brought you your coffee." Crooke pointed.

Donovan smiled at Megan who thought he wanted a refill and came over with the coffee pot.

"You found this girl Suzy?" Donovan put on his most trustworthy face.

"Me and Billy and his dad." Megan nodded.

"Can you spare a few minutes?"

Megan looked around, and seeing that all the customers were happy for the moment, sat down opposite Donovan, "Sure."

"You were at the dance; did you see anything untoward there?"

Megan shook her head, "Nah, the only trouble was after she went missing when a couple of guys were accusing each other of taking her."

"Do you know her well?" Donovan had closed his notebook as sometimes it put off the interviewee.

Again, Megan shook her head, "We said hello a few times at school, but she's two years below us, different circles."

"What do you know of her?"

Megan pulled a face, "She has a bit of a reputation for being easy, but I wouldn't give it much credit, people love to gossip."

"Can you describe how she was when you found her?"

"She was just wearing panties, and she was dirty, and her hair was full of twigs and leaves, just as though she had run through some bushes." She confirmed Crooke's evaluation.

"She was under a bush?" Donovan prompted.

"Oh yeah, she was real scared and mumbling, whimpering. It took us ages to coax her out," Megan nodded.

"What was she scared of?"

Megan shrugged, "I didn't see anything scary, but that was the following day and in daylight," she lifted her gaze up to Donovan, "I hope I'm never that scared!"

"Does anything about this make sense to you?"

Megan shook her head and then turned to Crooke, "Will she be alright?"

"We're keeping an eye on her, don't worry," Crooke stood and patted her shoulder, "I have to get back to work. Nice seeing you again Donovan."

The editor leant forward and spoke quietly to Megan, "Do you have any ideas of what happened, anything at all?"

Tears appeared in her eyes, "I just think that someone or something got to her. I know that she's a bit wild, but what happened doesn't make sense unless someone else was involved."

Donovan patted her arm, "If it's any comfort, that's how I feel."

After a few more words of comfort, he left and wandered back to his office. For some reason it troubled him; he felt that someone out there was responsible for the unfortunate girl's incident, and that was what troubled him, troubled him a lot!

White Tail Butte was a small, country town where people knew each other, and crime was restricted to occasional brawls and motoring offences, and major crime was virtually unknown. Not that this could be considered a major crime; nothing had happened and may have been self-inflicted, but if it wasn't, there was the threat of something disturbing, something lurking in the shadows.

Chapter Eight

Sheriff Reynolds would agree with Donovan's thoughts a few days later when he was called out to a grisly scene in the forest.

Old Hamish was an itinerant who appeared every summer and built a shelter in the woods, where he made a ferocious alcoholic brew from what he picked up from waste dumps and dustbins. The sheriff had expected that when he was called to the scene, it would be the result of Hamish's brew, at last getting the better of him, but it wasn't.

He was lying some distance from the lean-to that he called his summer home, and it was obvious that something had attacked him, a bear or a mountain lion the sheriff thought. His ragged clothes were torn, and most of his innards were hanging out, and his head had been smashed so hard that his brains had burst out.

The sheriff sighed; Hamish had been harmless and didn't need to be killed like this. He had been locked up overnight several times for being drunk and disorderly, but it was really to give him somewhere warm and dry to sleep and a hot meal. When he was sober, he revealed that he was surprisingly well educated, and the sheriff had enjoyed the conversations with him, but that wouldn't be happening anymore.

Sadly he walked back to his car and called the hospital and quickly got Crooke, "I'm out at the creek, and we got a nasty one Doc. Something has attacked Old Hamish and ripped him apart. Even I can see he's dead, but you had better come out and make it official."

He tramped back to the body and waved his arm towards the bushes, "Look round for any signs of what did this," he told his deputy. Then he walked over to the lean-to and peeked in. There were cans and bottles and a few books beside the camp bed, nothing else.

He was reading a book when Crooke arrived, who gave the corpse a cursory examination and unrolled the body-bag. He and the sheriff placed the body there and then carried it to the ambulance.

"Any idea of how long ago this happened?" Reynolds asked.

"I guess about a day; insects had started laying eggs, and something had been nibbling at his innards. Whatever did this was powerful," Crooke said as he shut the ambulance door, "it takes something to knock a brain out of its skull."

"Yeah, I reckon it was a bear, but I haven't seen one around here for years," Reynolds tipped his hat on to the back of his head, "but I haven't seen damage like that before either."

"I'll give him a proper examination and let you have the report."

"Thanks, Doc, I suppose the town will have to pay for his burial. More paperwork!" The sheriff called his deputy back, and after collecting the few possessions of Hamish they left the scene.

In the late afternoon, Crooke appeared in the sheriff's office.

"Hi Doc, you didn't have to bring the report yourself," The sheriff left his desk with a smile on his face which disappeared as he saw the serious expression on the doctor's face.

"I thought that I'd better come and explain my findings in person." The doctor looked very puzzled, "Old Hamish wouldn't have lived much longer as he had cancer everywhere, and his liver was more or less finished, but that wasn't what killed him, and I'm not sure if it was an animal."

"You saw the mess, it must have been an animal!" the sheriff objected.

"Well yes, the appearance was as if he had been attacked," Crooke paused, "Do you remember that I said it would take a powerful blow to knock out the brain? Well, there's no sign of a blow anywhere on the body, and especially the head, I looked very carefully."

The sheriff slowly sat down, "Are you saying this is a murder?"

Crooke shook his head rapidly, "I don't know what it is. It's as though the brain exploded out of the head, and what is also puzzling is that the stomach wasn't sliced open by a claw or anything like that, and also appears to have been pushed out."

"What could cause that?" Reynolds leant back in his chair.

"I wish I knew," Crooke took the other seat, "it's nothing in my experience, and I've spent hours on the internet and reading up, but there are no records of anything like it."

"There's no disease that does that? What about his drinking habits?"

"I don't know what he's been drinking, but if something caused internal pressure, the victim dies, and the process stops immediately. There's nothing that causes the pressure to continue," The doctor handed the sheriff the file, "I've recorded death by unknown reasons, and that's the first time I've ever done that!"

"Well, I was just going to put out a warning about dangerous wild animals," the sheriff took a deep breath, "I'll still do that, but I'll remove any mention of Hamish."

"I'll keep looking for a cause," Crooke rose and headed for the door, "if I find anything I'll let you know."

The sheriff read the file, and then stared at the closed folder on his desk. For a moment there he was feeling his stomach tense at the thought that it was a murder, perhaps it still was. Like the doctor, he didn't like loose ends.

Chapter Nine

Donovan didn't hear about Old Hamish for two days, and it would have been longer if he hadn't bumped into the sheriff in the Barbwire Grill where everyone seemed to take a morning break.

"It's stumped the Doc," the sheriff informed him.

"I'm not surprised if there no sign of being attacked, and the old boy was turned inside-out," Donovan picked up a pretzel and then put it down, "Do you think that it has anything to do with that girl Suzy?"

"They're both a bit weird, but the girl wasn't killed, and they happened at different times," the sheriff scratched his chin.

"She was almost scared to death," Donovan took a sip of coffee. "Something that could rip a body apart would be pretty scary."

"I didn't think that reporters were that sensitive," Reynolds commented.

The reporter put down his cup and studied the sheriff's face, as though making a judgement, "Most reporters change jobs after they have covered a really bad event, the rest of us learn to control our feelings for a while longer, but eventually we all seek other things to cover."

"Yeah, it's the same with policing," the sheriff nodded, "a lot of the bright young officers can turn to drink or worse after a few years, or just give up."

"What strikes me about this is that this town is a backwater, nothing happens here, but within a short time we have two strange incidents!"

"I thought the same, but I can't see a connection, except the forest and there's nothing there unless it's a savage squirrel!" The lawman stood up, "You should go over to the hospital and have words with Doc Crooke; he's tearing his hair out and would like someone to talk to."

Donovan slowly finished his coffee and bagel, thinking all of the while before sauntering down to the hospital. He found Crooke in his office with open books spread across the desk, and he looked as though he'd had too little sleep.

"You look worse than your patients!" Donovan lifted some books off a chair and sat down.

Crooke leant back and rubbed his face, "Thanks, it's nice to hear! You've heard about Old Hamish? It's a real puzzle, and I'm uneasy about not being able to find the cause of death."

"I thought that he was ripped apart," Donovan sat in a chair after removing some books.

"More like he exploded," the doctor passed a hand over the piles of books, "I've been looking for any other cases like this, and even into occult practices, but there is nothing that points the finger at the cause."

"What do you mean by 'exploded'?" Donovan took out his notebook.

"Just that, his organs appear to have been pushed out, but there are no cuts and no burns, the skin just split wide open," Crooke pushed his hair out of his eyes. "We did a complete screen on the contents of his stomach, and there was nothing there to create a tremendous pressure."

"Could I look at the body?" Donovan didn't relish the idea of viewing a mutilated body, but he'd seen his fair share over the years.

Crooke shook his head, "It's been sent to the morticians for disposal, but I took a lot of photographs. I should warn you that it's a mess," he reached for his laptop.

"It's okay; just show me what the puzzle is."

Crooke selected the file on his computer and displayed a shot of Hamish's head as it was found. Donovan winced at the sight.

"You can see that his brains have been almost totally pushed out, and this is what it looked like after I cleaned it up." The picture was replaced by one showing the brain completely removed and a gaping hole, "I shaved the head to look for any trauma, and there isn't one. Here's the other side."

Donovan studied the photographs, and he saw that there were no cuts, bruises or claw marks, "Surely it would have taken some force to push the brain out."

"Look at this." Crooke flicked up another view where the edges of the wound were pulled back, "the skull has been broken along the suture lines and pushed outwards, but still sticking to the skin."

"There's no bruising?" the reporter asked.

"Only some damage on the brain itself as it was pushed," the doctor produced another shot of Hamish's stomach, and Donovan felt his gorge rise. The internal organs were on the outside of the body.

"This is the same," Crooke changed to another shot of the organs removed, "this is not a cut, it's a split and the organs that remained inside had been displaced."

"And there's no illness that can do that?" Donovan paused in writing trying to find the words that could describe the injuries.

"Not in the time frame," Crooke looked at the reporter, "Did you ever talk to Hamish? He was brought in a few times, usually by the sheriff, and when he was sober he was as bright as a new pin; well-educated and a pleasure to talk to. Two days before his body was found, two ramblers had met him, and he was normal, at least for Hamish. There are things that can do this or something like it, but it would take weeks, months to produce internal pressure, and it would have been obvious; he would have complained of headaches and stomach pains."

"Was there anything else wrong with him?"

"He had jaundice, and that's not surprising because his liver was shot, and he had cancer. He would have been gone in a few months anyway."

"None of these things can cause death in this manner?" Donovan leant back and eased the sudden knot in his neck.

Crooke shook his head, "There would have been pain and discomfort, but nothing like this."

"There's no a tropical disease or exotic poisonous plants?" Donovan paused for a moment, "Could his drinking have caused this?"

"I've dealt with drunks before, and I've checked on other sources, and there is no evidence that anything can. Most of the really bad stuff kills almost immediately, and I've searched his lean-to for anything different. It's a total blank!" Crooke slapped the desk.

"I've seen something like this before," the reporter said thoughtfully, "It's caused by a shockwave. There was a guy in a wooden hut, and a bomb went off a few yards away, but the hut wasn't even scratched. When they opened the hut, the guy had been split open, similar to this. I understand that the blast is like a wavelength, and the hut was in the null position, but the poor guy was at the other extreme."

"There was no sign of an explosion," Crooke said but looked thoughtful, "It couldn't have been that, but thanks for the input."

"Just to change the topic slightly," Donovan wondered if he should ask, "Is there any links to that girl Suzy?"

Crooke though for a few moments before replying, "Not that I can see, except that something peculiar happened to both of them, but there are no similarities."

"Thanks, Doc, and if anything else turns up, really odd, please let me know." Donovan left the doctor, and both had a bad feeling.

Chapter Ten

With relief, Donovan returned to his normal routine. Most of the news was sent in from various affiliated agencies and just needed editing, but some needed a follow-up, sometimes just a 'phone call, but at other times it required a personal visit and a few photographs.

It was about a week later that he caught a bit of news from Medford. As part of a larger newspaper organisation, various bits and pieces would circulate the chain, and this one made him pause.

It concerned an old people's home in Medford where most of the inmates were suffering from dementia. An old lady by the name of Molly Barton, who had just celebrated her ninetieth birthday, had a remarkable remission. On the last day of being eighty-nine, she had been the same as she had been for many years, virtually a vegetable. On the first day of being ninety she was found walking along a corridor and looking for the toilet, and when she was approached by the staff she had let loose with language that would have made a sailor blush; this after years of not walking or saying a word.

It struck Donovan as being remarkable. As far as he knew, there was no remission from dementia as the brain had deteriorated to the point that it hardly could function. He needed an expert opinion, and he grabbed his jacket and headed for the hospital, clutching the report in his hand.

Crooke was in surgery with a patient, and Donovan had to wait.

"What's up?" the doctor emerged wiping his hands and noticed the reporter's impatience.

"What do you know about Alzheimer's?" Donovan demanded.

Crooke smiled, "Do you think you're going over the edge?"

"Frequently, and for most of my life, but what do you know?"

Crooke led him into his office, "Unfortunately, quite a lot and almost nothing. It's very common and increasing due to the numbers of older people. It would be great to find a cure or at least something to halt its progress. Why?"

Donovan thrust the report at him, "Read that and give me your opinion."

After quickly scanning the report, Crooke handed it back, "It could have been misdiagnosed, but after so many years she shouldn't have been able to function at all, whatever the cause."

"That's what I thought," Donovan frowned, "Would you like to come with me and see the old girl?"

"We'll have to ask first, but why the interest?" Crooke asked.

"It's something else that's peculiar, and my old nose smells a story," The reporter rubbed his nose.

"I'll give them a ring," Crooke reached for the telephone.

Medford's Old People Home looked cheerful enough from the outside. Donovan had expected something as run-down as the inmates. Doctor Philip Rogers was sceptical at first, but when Crooke produced his credentials, he gave in and talked freely.

"I didn't believe it when the sister called me; I was still having breakfast. Molly Barton has suffered from Alzheimer's for nearly twenty years, and for the last seven, she has been virtually a vegetable. I'll take you to see her, and you can judge for yourself, but if anything she is a bit lively. Her language makes even me blush!"

"Have you taken a scan of her since her recovery?" Crooke asked.

"Yeah, first thing, and I had one hell of a fight to get her there," he grinned at them, "I said that she was lively."

He took a file from a drawer and removed some plates and spread them out on the desk, "This is the one from twenty years ago, this one from twelve years ago and this one a month ago. The changes are obvious."

"When did she improve?" Donovan was scribbling notes.

"Just two months ago."

Crooke pulled the plates towards him, "These could have been taken in reverse order. I've never seen brain matter restored before. Do you have a CD copy of the scan?"

"Right here," Rogers swung the monitor round so that they could all see. From then on the two doctors used technical terms that lost Donovan, but he picked up a phrase here and there and continued scribbling until it was suggested that they should meet Molly and judge for themselves.

"Why don't you leave me alone? You're just a bunch of nosey buggers!" That was how Molly greeted them. Donovan covered a smile with his hand.

"Now, now Molly, we are interested in your case," Rogers attempted to placate her.

"There is no case; I'm feeling okay. There is nothing wrong with me!" she turned her face away from them.

"Being fit and healthy at ninety is just as interesting as being sick," Rogers tried to placate her.

"I'm eighty-nine, you dummy!" Molly waved her arms at them.

"You don't look it, Molly." She didn't. All of the other inmates were still in their pyjamas and dressing gowns. They had to be taken from place to place, or sit in an armchair with a blank expression. Molly was smartly dressed with a touch of make-up, and she had a fierce glint in her eye.

"You're just saying that 'cos you want something," Her face had a sly expression.

Rogers held his hands up, "Molly, we are just concerned about you, and don't want to see you relapse and become like these other folk."

"No chance! These are the people you should be concerned about. Do something with them!" Molly snapped and pointed to the other inmates.

Crooke tried to get through, "Molly, you got better, and we want to know how, and then we could possibly help the others."

"Mrs Barton to you! Who are you?" Molly's penetrating glare could have frightened the devil!

"I'm Dr Crooke, and I have a great interest in your case."

Molly looked at him, and he got the impression that he was dealing with a very shrewd lady.

"A whole gaggle of folk have prodded and poked at me, took pictures in a God awful machine, and finally took samples of blood and pee by the gallon. I don't want any more of that."

"We just want to talk," Rogers gave her a confident smile.

"Talk about what?" She calmed down a little and hugged her hands on her lap.

"Let's find a corner and sit down," Rogers led the way.

Having settled at a dining table, he continued, "For a long time you were like everyone else here. You had Alzheimer's, and no one has ever recovered from that before. If we can understand how that happened to you, we can help the others."

Crooke added his part, "Do you remember being slow like these other folk here, and then when you changed to what you are now?"

Molly gave him another sly look, "Now, that would be telling!"

Rogers tapped the folder, "We've all of the medical results and the reports from the staff here. What we don't have is what happened in your own words. It would help."

Molly pointed to Donovan with a skinny finger with a crimson lacquered nail, who had just put away his notebook, "Who's he?"

"That's Donovan; he's my associate, but not a doctor."

"Can I trust him?" Molly leant forward and glared into Donovan's face.

"He wouldn't be here if I didn't trust him. You can trust him too," Crooke had a brief thought as to whether the reporter was trustworthy.

"Well..." Molly looked from one to the other, "I do remember what it was like before. I could hear, but not understand what was going on. Sometimes I would be back in my home and talking to my husband, but then I would remember that he was killed in Italy. Then I would get all emotional, but I couldn't even cry."

Crooke leant forward, "That must have been very difficult for you."

"You betcha ass it was! The memories were as real to me as you are now. There is now even a part of me wondering if you're real."

Rogers chuckled and touched Molly's hand, "We're real. I suppose living in memories one moment, and today the next moment was very confusing."

Molly just nodded and looked out of the window. There was a hint of a tear in her eyes.

"What happened when you recovered?" Molly shot Donovan a look as if to wonder why he would ask such a question.

"I had a dream," her voice became very soft, and they all leant forward to hear better, "I had a dream, I was sitting in a forest, and it was springtime or early summer, and the world smelled fresh. I could feel a warm breeze and hear the bees humming. There was a woodpecker over my head."

"That's it? There was nothing else?" Rogers looked at the others, "this is the first time I've heard this."

"I woke up feeling my bladder bustin!" Molly regained her usual boisterous attitude.

Donovan looked puzzled, "Let me get this straight. You were in a confused state of mind; you went to bed, had a dream and woke up in a normal state."

"You got it kid!" Molly punched the air.

Crooke looked just as puzzled, "Can you remember the previous week or so?"

"Clearly, I can remove all the old stuff, and what's left is what really happened."

"What did you do in that week?" Crooke asked.

"We went on a trip on our old bus, and had afternoon tea at a place somewhere; I can't remember where. Old Charlie over there had a birthday on the following day, and we had cake. Missy had a stroke, I think two days afterwards, and you came to her,"

Rogers nodded in agreement, "The rest of the time it was the usual routine. I wish they wouldn't show us those soap operas; they are so stupid, but I like that crime series, all of them."

Rogers sat back and smiled at her, "Molly, there is nothing wrong with your memory."

"I know that, but just tell these idiots!" Molly gestured towards Crooke and Donovan.

They left Molly giving a nurse a chunk of her mind and sat in Crooke's car. Crooke held up the CDs Rogers had given him, "I'm going to study these a bit more, but even now I can tell you that this is definitely weird! Her brain cells were rebuilt overnight, not a week or a month, overnight! It's impossible!"

"How does that fit in with the other weird things?" Donovan asked.

Crooke shook his head, "It doesn't! Molly regained her mind; Suzy lost hers, and poor Old Hamish died. I can't see any connection!"

"You mean that the different end results do not have a common factor?" Donovan wrote a couple of words and then put the notebook away.

"Yeah and while we're here in Medford, there's another home I want to visit. I've already been in contact with them." Crooke started the car's engine.

Chapter Eleven

Timmy Bateman was a darling boy. At ten years of age, he should have been able to go out and play with the other children, but autism is a strange and sad affliction that is not fully understood by specialists and lay alike. Adults were confused, and children more often than not hurled verbal and physical abuse because they did not understand, and what you do not understand, you fear.

Timmy's parents took him to a special school in Medford every Monday morning and left him until the Friday. The trained staff could look after Timmy's needs, and allow Mr and Mrs Bateman to lead fairly normal lives. Even with grants, it cost a fortune, and with well-paid jobs, the Bateman's could just afford to keep Timmy at the school.

One aspect of autism is that the sufferers have the ability of great concentration. Timmy could be set a task and left alone while he completed the task to perfection. Then he needed a hug and praise before the next task. It was rare, but sometimes the autistic children would spontaneously cooperate in a task. No one understood why.

Jenny Kraft looked at the autistic kids playing in the garden. Officially she had been doing this for nearly fifteen years, but before that she had experience with an autistic cousin. When she was small, he frightened her with his grunts for speech and his shambling gait. If she had known the word at that age, she would have said that he was a Neanderthal. As it was, he scared the daylights out of her!

As she grew older, she realised by the love and affection of his parents that he was, unfortunately special. From that point on she became absorbed in the subject of autism, and ended up in the special school in Central Point, just outside Medford.

Her present preoccupation was to spot anything unusual where unusual was the norm. Most of the kids typically rocked back and forward, and those walking looked more like chameleons; a hesitant back and forward step as they traversed the garden.

What caught her attention was Timmy, sitting against the fence with his head back and staring blankly at the sky. He was perfectly motionless, but that happened sometimes.

Jenny casually walked in that direction, talking to the other kids as she passed them. The one thing you are not supposed to do was to create a disturbance. Eventually, she was standing next to Timmy, and for a terrible moment she thought he was dead; there was no sign of breathing, but then she saw that his chest was rising and falling very slowly, unusually slow.

She knelt down beside him, "Timmy, can you hear me? What are you doing?"

It was a fifty-fifty chance that he would respond. He didn't, so she sat down and took his hand and squeezed it gently. His fingers moved slightly. Good, he wasn't drifting completely away. Curt Vagens, the senior male attendant, saw what she was doing and casually walked over.

"We got a problem?"

Jenny shook her head, "I think that he's just day-dreaming. I'll sit here until he stops."

"I've seen these kids do this for a day or two. If he's still out at the end of the shift, we'll have to bring him out of it," Curt frowned; when they were forced to do something these kids could become violent, and they had no sense of pain. He'd known them to walk on broken legs!

At the end of her shift, Jenny stood up still holding Timmy's hand. Surprisingly, he stood up with her while still looking at the sky. Slowly she led him back into the school and laid him on a cot. She bent over and kissed him on the forehead. It usually got a response, but not this time. Jenny shrugged and looked up at Curt.

"I think that we should just leave him to come out by himself. I'll tell the night crew."

"If he's still like that in the morning, we'll have to take action," but Curt did not have to. The night staff kept a vigilant eye on Timmy, and it was noticed that eventually, his eyes were closed, and his breathing became normal.

Jenny started her shift the next morning to see if Timmy was awake and ready for breakfast. She found him smiling up at her from the bed, "Good morning Timmy."

"Good morning Jenny," the words came easily, and she took a moment for them to register.

Stammering, she came closer, "H - how are you this morning?" She could hardly believe her ears, but she also had to act normally.

"I'm fine. How are you?" Timmy gave her a bright smile.

Tears flowed out of her eyes unchecked.

Crooke asked for Jenny when they arrived, and they were directed into the garden. Crooke introduced himself and Donovan and then reminded her of their telephone conversation.

"I remember, and it's good of you to come out here," Jenny shook their hands, "It's a marvellous thing to have happened; would you like to meet Timmy?"

"Just fill us in on a few details first," Crooke pulled her gently back, "Have you been conducting any unusual programs here, a different drug regime, that sort of thing?"

Jenny gave a small smile, "Not a thing, you can check the records if you like. We just look after the kids, and there are no special programs. He's over there."

Timmy was playing with another boy and talking to him. The other boy may have been listening, but appeared not to be paying attention to the words or the play.

Jenny bent over them, "Timmy, these gentlemen want to talk to you. Can you spare the time?"

"Oh sure, Johnny's not all that keen on this," He stood up without any difficulty and looked up at the two visitors, "Are you doctors?"

"I'm a doctor Timmy, my name is Crooke, and this is my friend Donovan," Crooke held out his hand, and the boy shook it, and did the same for the reporter. The handshake was firm.

"I suppose you want to know what happened," Timmy looked and sounded like any normal child, but still retained the directness that was so common with autistic children.

"Do you know what happened?" Crooke asked.

Timmy shook his head, "Huh, huh, I woke up in my room and things seemed different," he smiled up at Jenny, "then Jenny came in and said 'Good morning', that's all I know."

"What do you remember of the previous day?" Crooke continued his line of questioning.

Timmy frowned and looked uncomfortable, "It's a bit of a muddle, bits and pieces that are all jumbled up."

Donovan had a hunch, "Did you have a dream?"

"Oh yeah, it was like being in a long darkness and flashing lights. It went on for a long time." Timmy frowned and looked uncertain, "I think that I have had that dream several times."

Crooke shot the reporter a puzzled look but continued his questions. "What do you mean by 'a long darkness'?"

Timmy concentrated, "It was like a tunnel, but it wasn't a tunnel and very wide."

"How do you feel today?" Crooke automatically took the boy's hand to check the pulse.

"Oh I feel great, but I have to leave here soon and go to another school. I'll miss Jenny." The boy looked down at his feet.

Jenny bent down and hugged him, "You're not to worry about that, you'll make lots of new friends, and I'll come to see you often."

"Really?" Timmy looked up and revealed the tears he had been shedding.

Crooke thought that they had heard enough, "Thanks for talking to us Timmy, it's been a real pleasure, now perhaps you should go over and play with Johnny again."

He watched as Timmy walked back to his friend, and noticed that it was not like the usual shambling gait that he associated with autistics.

Chapter Twelve

"Where have you two been?" The sheriff greeted them as they pulled up at the hospital.

"Donovan wanted my expert opinion about something," Crooke was surprised at the officer's manner, and didn't feel like supplying any details, "What's happened?"

"Walk down to my office; there's someone who needs to talk to you," The sheriff walked off and didn't wait to see if they were following.

Inside his office, a tall blonde woman stood up as they entered. The sheriff waved them forward, "This is Special Agent Elizabeth Hanningford, FBI. This is Doctor Crooke and Michael Donovan."

"What's this about?" Donovan wondered what he had done to attract the FBI's attention, but then again he thought that he didn't mind the attention from such a strikingly beautiful woman.

"Old Hamish," the sheriff grunted without elaboration.

"Don't tell me he was an international terrorist!" Donovan smiled at his jest, but neither the sheriff nor the agent returned the smile.

"I just want to know what you know of him," the agent's voice was seductively soft and low.

"I never met him, but Crooke and the sheriff have," Donovan wondered what this was about.

"He was a surprisingly well educated but unfortunate man," Crooke supplied.

"How well educated? Where was he educated?" the agents gaze focused on the doctor, "and why unfortunate?"

"I don't know where he was educated, but I get the impression that some of it was somewhere abroad, maybe England, and I think that his subject was history." Crooke felt uncomfortable under the gaze of those icy blue eyes, "I just got the impression that something bad had happened in the past."

"That agrees with what the sheriff found in his lean-to." The agent indicated a pile of stuff on the sheriff's desk.

"What's this all about?" Donovan was worried that something was wrong, and he hoped that they had not stepped on anyone's toes, "Doc here did the autopsy and ended up with some strange results, but there was no foul play as far as we could make out."

"I have the records and photographs, but the body was sent for dispatch weeks ago," Crooke defended himself.

The agent briefly shook her head, "We know - and we have the body now. It's those strange results that concern us."

Crooke was dumbfounded! He had never had anyone question his work before, and usually, if there was a question they came to him first, "We sent off samples for testing, but they didn't reveal a positive answer."

"We know, and we don't have any different ideas than you came up with," the agent smiled to take the tension out of the air, "that's why I'm here. We need some more information. Please sit down, this isn't an interrogation."

"I don't know what we can add," Crooke said, "the sheriff had most to do with him, and I only met him when the sheriff brought him in, mainly for a free bed and a hot meal."

"I've looked at the sheriff's and the hospital's records, and you enter him as just 'Old Hamish'; that's a Scottish name isn't it? Do you know his last name?"

"No, he never mentioned it, even when pressed." Crooke pursed his lips before adding, "It's Gaelic, and so it could also be Irish or even Canadian. There are a lot of Scots in Canada."

"Or American; we're looking at immigration records to find a Hamish with a better than average education," the agent looked up from her notes, "How old do you think he is?"

"In his fifties, maybe sixty at the most," Crooke looked relieved, "he looked a lot older."

"What's behind your investigation?" Donovan asked.

"We're always on the lookout for a new virus in case there's an epidemic, and we just want to find this case a home since it's so unusual." Hanningford closed her notebook, "Now, if you don't mind, can we look and discuss your records?"

As they walked out of the door, Donovan looked back and saw that the sheriff was more than usually worried, his face creased in something almost approaching pain. He had serious concerns about something, most probably that the FBI was on his turf!

Chapter Thirteen

Megan became one of the boys. She attached herself to Billy, and usually, there were at least one of the other boys, and she started to get a reputation as the gang's 'moll' by the most conservative members of the community, and the more jealous students. It was Marcus who explained her change of behaviour.

"Look at the guys; they're all jocks, except me, and I think that she feels safer with them. I certainly wouldn't like to tackle any of them on a dark night or any other time, and I feel safe with them, but what surprises me as that they tolerate me being around. They're good guys!"

That was something that Donovan picked up on during his daily round of news gathering. The citizens of White Tail Butte weren't scared, but they were certainly apprehensive. The town had changed from a sleepy backwater where nothing remarkable happened, to one where there was an expectancy of further events, a sense of caution and strangers were given a second look, a thoughtful look.

He sat in the sheriff's office and mentioned what he felt.

"Well yes, I'm not surprised that folk have changed," the sheriff said as he mulled over the question, "when that girl disappeared we all had expectations that a rape or murder had occurred, and it was an anti-climax when she was found relatively safe. That initial feeling never fully went away, and it was reinforced with the death of Old Hamish."

"It's not an obvious change, more like a feeling," the reporter replied. "No one has said that there is a sense of danger, but there is an expectation of – something."

"Like Christmas!" The sheriff smiled.

"That's a very good analogy," Donovan smiled at the sheriff's joke, "It's as though there is something coming, and they're excited or frightened at the prospect."

The sheriff eyed the town reporter, all humour gone from his face. He came to a decision.

"Donovan, you've been in a few tight spots in the past, and you know when to keep your mouth shut. Can you keep another secret, and I mean really secret!"

Surprised at the sudden change of subject, Donovan hesitated. The last time he had heard these words was in Sarajevo, and the thought made him apprehensive. He and every other reporter were told not to mention certain things.

"If it's illegal or immoral, I'll have to say something, but I think that it's something to do with these weird goings-on. Of course, I won't cause a panic."

"This stays within these walls. There've been more incidents!" The sheriff looked nervously at the door.

Donovan sat bolt upright, "Where? I haven't heard anything."

The sheriff waved his hand dismissively, "Not around here, and that's why the FBI were interested. Something is going on, and she wasn't all that forthright with me. I found out through the grapevine."

"Does Crooke know?" Donovan's face matched the seriousness of the sheriffs.

"Not yet, but some reports will filter down to him through the medical grapevine eventually. I'll have to warn him to keep quiet as well." Reynolds leant forward and scribbled a reminder on a notepad.

"What can you tell me of these other incidents?" Donovan produced his notebook. He hadn't used it so much for years.

"After the FBI had left, I made a few 'phone calls and it's more or less what happened here; people were acting strange like Suzy, and a few unexplained deaths."

"How many incidents?" Donovan was writing furiously.

The sheriff looked down at his hands that lay on the desk, "Thirty-five and counting,"

"Thirty-five! Is it a person doing these things? The public have to be told!" Donovan's face grew grim.

"Not a word, remember! You've seen some of the evidence, and there's nothing to pin on anyone or anything, so I'll deny anything you say, and the FBI will close you down. I just want you not to be surprised and go off half-cocked and cause a panic." Reynolds waved a warning finger at the reporter.

Donovan settled back in his chair, "Yeah, there is no connection between Hamish and Suzy, as far as we know. Did you read that article about the old lady recovering from Alzheimer's?"

"Yes I did, and Agent Hanningford noticed similar things elsewhere, in fact, she picked up on unusual occurrences as you did."

"There was another one in Medford, an autistic boy who became normal overnight, absolutely normal." Donovan started to search his pockets, and then remembered that he had stopped smoking five years earlier. He could do with one now!

"Why is the FBI interested in weird events?" Donovan pointed out the obvious, "This is all medical stuff unless there is more to it than she is telling."

"All very mysterious," the sheriff stood up, "Want to come with me and see Crooke? This seems to be more in his field than ours."

"Does the mayor know any of this?"

"Now there's one hell of a nervous guy; what do you think?" The sheriff clamped his hat on firmly.

Chapter Fourteen

It didn't take Donovan long to check out the sheriff's story, just a few 'phone calls to the editors of similar newspapers that he had met over the years. He would casually introduce the story of Old Hamish and wait for a response, and there were more than he expected; there were even a few incidents like Suzy's, but could also have been attempted rapes. On a hunch, he mentioned to the editor in Illinois about Molly's rejuvenation and received information of three similar occurrences.

It took him all day, and he looked at his notepad at the end and decided that he needed to think about what to do. Deep in thought, he headed across the road for the Barbed Wire Grill; perhaps some fresh coffee and a hot meal would give him some inspiration.

Lost in thought, he ordered on autopilot and only became aware of the noise as he looked for somewhere to sit. The boys, including Megan, were horsing around in the far corner, and the noise was mainly laughter.

"Do you mind if I sit in with you?" They made way for him in surprise, but without any undue rancour.

"What's happening Mister Donovan?" Megan asked.

"Mike please or just Donovan! My father is Mister Donovan, and he departed from this world many years ago."

"Where do you come from Donovan?" Billy asked.

"I was born in Dublin, but my folks moved to New York soon after."

"Begorrah! You're from the auld country!" Sean put on what he thought was an Irish accent.

"You're Sean, right?" the reporter fixed him with a steely gaze, "With that name you're not far from there yourself."

"Ah, 'tis the truth you'll be saying," Sean wasn't fazed by the stare.

"So what is happening out in the world?" Megan repeated.

Donovan's dinner arrived, and he was surprised to find that he'd ordered a burger, and the interruption gave him time to think what to answer. "You tell me, I just collect things."

"Joel used to collect stamps, and Gerry collected matchsticks, until he burned them," Sean revealed.

"I should not have used live matches!" Gerry said sadly.

"Do you see that girl -," Donovan pretended not to remember the name, "Suzy something that had that trouble?"

"Not much, just at school," Megan pulled a face, "Her parents keep her pretty close to home now, and she hardly speaks to anyone since then. I guess she's still scared."

"What do you make of that, now that you've had time to think?" Donovan took a sip of coffee. It was too hot, and he replaced it on the saucer quickly!

"I think that something scared her half to death," Megan said quietly, "something a lot worse than we see in the horror movies!"

"I spoke to her a few days ago," Billy thoughtfully focused on the subject, "She didn't appear to remember that anything happened, or perhaps she just doesn't want to talk about it."

"Has anyone else heard of any other silly things like that?" Donovan took a mouthful of burger and waited. A good reporter needs patience to gather a story.

Megan frowned, "I wouldn't call that 'silly'; to her, it must have been a terrible experience."

Donovan gulped down the mouthful, "Okay, I'll accept that. Shall we use the term peculiar?"

Marcus sat opposite Donovan with a good view of everyone, and he had been looking closely at the reporter, "Why the interest Mister Donovan?"

"I told you, just Donovan! Nothing in particular, I was just being a nosey reporter."

"I read that article you wrote about that autistic boy; that was peculiar!" The young man's stare never broke away from Donovan's face.

'Blast! Marcus was by far the most intelligent of the group, and had apparently seen through my line of questioning', Donovan thought as he tried to deflect the question.

"It was peculiar, and there are no known explanations. Did you also see the article about the old lady in Medford who recovered from Alzheimer's? The unusual and inexplicable catch my attention, and they make good news." The reporter took a bite of the burger.

"So you just want to know if we'd heard of anything peculiar." Billy looked round the table, "Joel forgot where he lived, and made a mess of his old man's store."

Joel scowled at Billy, "It was some bad beer or that poison oak; I was alright after a couple of days."

"You looked horrible the day after, "Megan nudged his arm, "You came in here and looked like a ghost."

"Oh yeah, I forgot that!" Billy's face lit up, "You never have sugar in coffee, but you filled the cup and ate my pie as well as yours."

"I did?" Joel's expression was one of genuine surprise. Obviously, he had forgotten.

"You had three portions of pie," Megan reminded him, "I know you're a big guy, but that was a bit over the top!"

"Tell me about the bad beer," Donovan sat back to listen, but from the corner of his eye, he saw that Marcus was still staring at him.

"Every year, at the start of the holidays we go out and camp for the weekend. At first, it was something with our folks, but the last couple of years it's just us," Billy explained.

"I didn't go," Megan looked superior, "They act like pigs!"

Billy nodded, "It's a bit silly and wild, but we want to let off steam. Anyway, this year we planned to see Crater Lake, and we took some beer. The tent collapsed overnight, and we had walked into something like poison oak; we were scratching for a couple of days. We weren't fit to drive, and we just managed to see the lake for an hour or so before driving home."

Gerry broke in, "We nearly didn't get home. Joel was driving, and he became lost on the outskirts of town; most weird! Anyway, the following day we both went to the store to help out, but we both got confused and ended up making a helluva mess. It took us days to put it right."

Joel nodded, "I remember the store fiasco. I don't know why that happened, and I still say it was the beer."

"Both you and Gerry were affected, no one else?" Donovan looked at the others, "What about the itching?"

"It was murder!" Gerry pulled a face, "Just the hands and arms, and it lasted about two days."

"It couldn't have been poison oak or ivy as we had no rashes or spots," Marcus still stared at Donovan, "It was more like a dose of itching powder, but no one here would do that, would we?" The others shook their heads and gave mock denials.

Donovan smiled as he looked at them. In some ways they were an odd bunch, Billy and Sean were obviously the centre with Joel giving his massive support, while Gerry hovered around them like a satellite. Marcus was the odd one; nothing butch about him with his glasses sliding down his skinny nose. Megan offered the group some stability and seemed to fit in at all levels. They were good natured youngsters that wouldn't harm anyone he decided.

Chapter Fifteen

"I've managed to get some reports on the other incidents," Donovan had called a council of war with the sheriff and Crooke in the sheriff's office. "Unfortunately, they're not very technical, and I can't see a connection except that they are weird."

"Well, we haven't got very much technical stuff as it is," Crooke held out his hand, "Show us what you have."

"I've made copies for you both," Donovan held out two folders.

Sheriff Reynolds took the file with an obvious distaste for its contents. He had already been warned that it contained reports of death and strange behaviour, but outside of his jurisdiction. Despite that, he felt that he should do something more than reading about them.

Crooke didn't appear to have any such doubts and starting leafing through the sheets, giving each a brief glance before moving to the next. Donovan just sat back and waited until both had finished.

The sheriff read more slowly and punctuated the silence with occasional "My God!" or "Jeez!" as each horror, and abnormal behaviour was revealed, but eventually he read the last sheet and closed the folder, and then looked up at the other two.

"If all this had happened in one town, there would be a general hue and cry, and people are demanding that something be done," he stated.

"The questions are," Donovan ticked off on his fingers," is there a connection to all of these, if so, what is causing it, and finally, what can we do? We can't do the last without answering the first two."

Crooke had been shuffling his papers, "I've sorted them into categories. These are like Molly and Timmy and possibly include the boys here. These are those like Suzy, and these are like Hamish." He had one more bunch in his hand, "These are something different again, and they're the most disturbing!"

Donovan took the papers and looked at them, "Yeah, I noticed these and wondered what you'd think of them," then he passed them to the sheriff, who looked at them.

"They all seem nuts to me! Why have you singled them out?" he snorted and handed the folder back.

Crooke leant forward, "You're right in that they are nuts. These are people who have simply lost their minds, either for a day or for good."

"Apart from the deaduns, they don't look different than the rest," the sheriff blew out his cheeks and sighed, "What is special about them Doc?"

Crooke took back papers, "This one is a young man, in his twenties, who forgot who his wife and kids were or where he lived. This one is a young woman who went berserk with an axe, but fortunately, didn't hurt anyone. This one is an old man who insists that a child belongs to him and from this record, he was never married. An arts teacher starts spouting advanced mathematics and so on."

"As I said, they're nuts!"

"I'll have to remember that technical term!" Donovan said and pretended to write it down.

"Have you checked any further on these?" Crooke aimed the question at the reporter.

Donovan shook his head, "I was just talking about the daft things people do and didn't want to bring undue attention to my questions."

"Good, I'm going to ask some of my colleagues in these towns, and also try to keep a low profile. We'll meet again when I have some more information," Crooke sounded positive.

"What about the FBI?" Donovan asked the sheriff.

"I haven't heard anything from her, but I know they're still looking; they never give up!" The sheriff hoisted his gunbelt, "What do you want me to do, apart from waiting?"

"Can you casually ask around in those towns, make up some dumb story about some guy you're looking for?" Crooke advised.

"Yeah I can, and I don't have to give any reason." He gave them a wicked grin.

"Just don't make anyone more curious than they have to be," Donovan advised.

Chapter Sixteen

Special Agent Elizabeth Hanningford hadn't given up, but she had nearly dropped the ball. She and her team had been monitoring press reports and police reports, but there is another team that records telephone conversations, e-mails and mobile and radio messages. It's a part of the anti-terrorist group that feeds information not just to the FBI but to the CIA, and even the British MI6 and others around the world.

That team leader, Jason Bailey realized that there may be a connection to Elizabeth's investigation and some of the messages that were flagged, and he gave her the 'head's up'.

"I don't know if this is anything to do with your sniffing around, but you had better check them out, they are the oddest reports I've ever seen!" he dumped a pile of CDs on her desk and left.

She smiled as she read the report on Donovan's casual chats to colleagues on other newspapers, and within a few days she was reading about Sheriff Reynolds and Crooke's conversations by telephone and e-mail.

She wasn't surprised as she thought that Crooke and Donovan were smart cookies. She also realised that sooner or later someone else would start to wonder about odd things. There were so many cranks out there who thought everything was a conspiracy; Elizabeth had to deal with those from time to time, but these two were not cranks, and would not satisfied with any diversions. She was annoyed that the sheriff had taken them into his confidence, our confidence, without asking her first!

It was time for another visit!

Crooke and Donovan were called to the sheriff's office early in the morning and were not completely surprised to see Special Agent Hanningford waiting for them. She was sitting in the sheriff's chair and leaning forward on the sheriff's desk. The sheriff was seated on one of the visitor's chairs, and looking uncomfortable at being displaced. It was obvious that the agent had given him a rough time about security.

"Good morning boys, made any 'phone calls lately?" She held up the file that Donovan had given the sheriff.

"Ah, it's not what you think," Donovan produced an almost convincing smile, "I thought that something was a bit odd, and Crooke thought so about a couple of other things. It was only natural that we looked into it and dragged in Reynolds."

"I was pissed when I found out that you had been asking questions, but when I read this," the agent tapped the folder, "I think I may have made a mistake. I was struck by the stories about the boy's camping trip, and the old lady and the autistic boy. We missed those."

"You would have," Crooke calmly took another seat, "The camping trip wasn't anything peculiar, most kids get out of town at the first opportunity, and Donovan only found out through a casual conversation, and I found out about Timmy through my usual contacts. I wasn't looking for anything at the time."

"It was you coming here in the first place that switched on my radar," Donovan took the only other chair left, "I would have shelved it in the silly files if you hadn't turned up!"

"So I'm to blame," Elizabeth nodded slightly, "You're probably right, but who else have you told?"

"No one and we tried to keep anyone's curiosity switched off," Donovan replied, "How did you hear about what we were doing?"

"We have our ways, and there is such a thing as Homeland Security," she replied.

"You spied on us?" Crooke pulled a face.

"Not intentionally, certain key words are fed into a computer, and when they occur, warnings flare up," the agent studied them, "You obviously used one or more of those words, and the operator was astute enough to realise that I would be interested. Otherwise, you would have gone undetected. About ninety-nine percent of what we pick up is of no interest to anyone. I have a nephew who texts things that set off the alarms nearly every day!"

"Okay, you've found us out, now what?" Donovan tried to look nonchalant, but his heartbeat had risen a notch or three.

"Nothing! I could roast your hides, but you've kept it quiet and produced some extra and interesting results," she turned to Crooke, "What do you make of all this Doctor?"

"I've managed to get some files, but they show nothing unusual. What is needed is really detailed examinations, but that would raise questions."

"What sort of examinations?" Elizabeth asked.

Crooke ticked off on his fingers, "Well, nearly all these show an unusual neural activity, and that means brain scans, IQ tests, motor response, that sort of thing. It would be too obvious that something was up."

Elizabeth picked up the folder and considered it for a few minutes, and then laid it down carefully, "If we can't hide it, we'll have to bury it in something obvious."

"Such as?" Crooke looked thoughtful.

"Your scuttling around here is too obvious as everyone knows you," the agent looked at the ceiling, "It will have to come from the top, some program that would include our subjects as well as others."

"A version of 'find the lady'!" Donovan grunted, referring to a card game.

"How can we do that?" Sheriff Reynolds asked.

"I'll have to go back to the office and storm their brains," Elizabeth smiled brightly, "it's marvellous what can be done when you really put your mind to it!"

"What shall we do in the meantime?" Donovan uncoiled himself and stood up.

"Just keep listening. There's no need to ferret around for details; we can do that from base without raising any questions. Now, is there a decent place for some food, I'm ravenous!"

Chapter Seventeen

It was over a week later that Donovan received a plain brown envelope from Elizabeth.

'Dear Donovan,

You will hear of an accident that will cause an investigation into the health of the population, please take it at face value. We will 'crash' a military aircraft in a remote area, and there are risks of 'exposure to radiation'.

We thought of several ways to start Crooke's idea, and this seems to be the best way. We cannot afford to examine everyone, and there will be questions raised in the Senate as to why some areas are left out. Politicians will interfere with every well-intentioned plan!

There will be questions as to why the plane crashed, and why it was carrying nuclear material, but that is what they do, so it is easier to handle.

There will also be a low-key exercise in testing schoolchildren in some areas for odd results. This is where the 'crash' investigation cannot go, and we cannot 'crash' several aircraft.

I will see you in a few days,

Best Wishes

Elizabeth Hanningford

PS. There are nearly 400 cases over a very wide area.

Donovan sat back in his chair. It wasn't surprising that the FBI could do this, after all, they could infiltrate most places, and the CIA could create any situation to fit any scenario that would suit their purpose. This would have been a simple exercise for any of them.

He stuffed the letter into a pocket and walked over to the hospital. Without saying a word, he placed it in Crooke's hand.

"Well, they haven't wasted much time!" Crooke re-read the letter, "It doesn't say when they'll start, but school commences in two weeks; just in time. This crash will be perfect as no one is going to object to safety procedures."

"What about the dead bodies we have so far, can't they examine those?"

"What about them?" Crooke shrugged, "We need a live body to test it, and unless you can come up with an idea of how to find someone just before they have an attack, it's a no go."

"How are they going to do this?" Donovan took the letter back, "They can't use the existing facilities!"

"I would think that it will be mobile test centres," Crooke considered the idea, "We can't have hordes of people invading hospitals; we would grind to a halt, and that would create a lot of complaints from people with normal complaints."

The official notification duly arrived via the mayor's office and Donovan was invited over to the Civil Centre to obtain more details. The mayor welcomed him with pleasure.

Thomas Edgerton was exactly what you would expect a mayor to be; corpulent, cheerful and optimistic to the point of idiocy. "Come in, Michael," he always used Donovan's first name, "You're just in time for morning coffee. I suppose that you want something on these school tests?"

"Yes, I want to know what you think of them." Donovan sat in an easy chair and the mayor took the other with a coffee table between them.

"About time they looked into this intelligence stuff; it never made much sense to me but putting it on a firm scientific footing will produce remarkable results, you'll see." The mayor waited impatiently for Donovan to select the first cake.

Donovan smiled, thinking that if the mayor knew what was behind the tests, he would be shocked into silence. Far from becoming quiet, Donovan's smiled encouraged him to go further.

"This country is slipping behind the rest of the world! Where are the marvellous brains that produced the motorcar or even nuclear energy?" His forefinger thumped heavily on his blotter.

" I thought that it was the German Jews and English that did most of the groundwork on nuclear energy and the Germans invented the car!" Donovan kept the smile on his face.

"But they came here, to Princeton and Los Alamos where they could work!" The mayor's speech was halted as his secretary brought in the coffee.

"As I was saying, they came here where they had freedom to think and work. We need to find those people again and lead us to tomorrow's bright future."

"Can I use that phrase? It would make a great headline." Donovan scribbled in his notebook.

"What phrase? Oh, you mean tomorrow's bright future; yes, it does have a ring to it. Use it all, my boy, and please do have a cake."

Donovan eventually left there with his notebook full of optimistic quotes and sticky fingers. His next port of call was the principal of the high school.

Hugh Pritchard was more pessimistic than the mayor. "What I can't see is what they expect to achieve." He had taken the post just three years before and had brought positive changes to the school and curriculum that Donovan approved of. Pritchard was ex-military, Donovan thought that it was Navy, and he needed a fighting spirit to fight the dull-minded opposition that he had found in the town.

"Surely, if they can isolate the reasons why some achieve good results and some not, it would be a good thing. Why is it that two brothers can be at opposite ends of the intelligence spectrum?" Donovan put forward one of the mayor's points.

"It may not lay in clinical causes," Pritchard took up a pencil and twirled it in his fingers, "A long time ago there were arguments about nature and nurture, and then we started to find out about genes. There are genetic reasons for differences in siblings, but that doesn't mean that one of them is less intelligent. We all have talents, and the objective of a school is to bring out those talents, but at the same time, we can't all be Einsteins; we have to give thought to the Frank Lloyd Wrights and Rembrandts as well. It's no accident that da Vinci was an engineer, a scientist and an artist. We specialise too much without giving scope to different aspects of life."

"Wow! You have given this some thought!" Donovan agreed with him, but had to remain neutral, "But I thought that the more knowledge we can put into the question, the better the answers would become."

Pritchard waved the pencil, "Don't get me wrong; all knowledge is important, but I want to know what they are expecting. If they want to prove a point, the results can be biased."

"Fudging the exam?" Donovan asked.

"Exactly! What was that guy's name? It'll come to me in a minute. He produced the first useable IQ test, and thousands of people all over the world used that test to decide their futures, but after he had died it was found that his data was false. He thought that he was from the intelligent sector and fixed the data based on white Anglo-Saxon, middle-class males of a decent education; exactly what he was."

"I know the story," Donovan closed his notebook, "One of the first questions against it was what if a person can't read or write; there's no way they can complete the test, but many were found to be very intelligent."

"Cyril Burt, that was the guy's name," Pritchard looked pleased that he remembered, "An English guy and his work was brought into disrepute, and there are continual arguments about it. A lot of it is certainly in error!"

"I thought all psychology could be argued."

"That's my point!" Pritchard tapped his desk with the pencil, "There are so many variables that it's impossible to draw the same conclusion twice, and good science demands that it has to be proved more than once."

"What you're saying is that we are all individuals and we can't fit them all into a standard test."

"That's it! I want to know what the expectations are before I come to a conclusion about these tests," Pritchard threw down his pencil.

Donovan had one more interview to make before he settled down to write the article and he waited for the subjects to appear. His office was almost opposite the Barbed Wire Grill, and he kept an eye on the entrance while he worked.

He saw Megan, Billy and Sean enter the Grill first, and the others came a few minutes later. He put on his jacket and crossed the street.

"Hi Mister Donovan, how are you today?" Megan asked brightly.

"I keep telling you, no 'mister' and I'm okay thank you, how are you all?" Donovan sat next to her.

"Just fine except we're back to school next week," Joel said gloomily.

"Have you heard about some tests that they're going to give you?" Donovan asked.

"Yeah, and it gives me the creeps," Sean muttered, "People reading my mind."

"In your case, they'd never publish what they find," Billy ducked as Sean tried to hit his head.

"Worse than that," Gerry crossed his eyes, "What if they turned us into zombies?"

"They'll never notice the difference in you," Megan giggled.

"All kidding aside, are you worried about it?" Donovan looked concerned.

"I am and not because I believe in mind-reading or zombies," Marcus pushed his glasses back up his nose, "Why are they doing it? I've read a lot about IQ tests and all of the arguments, and none of it means beans."

"Do you know what sort of tests they're planning?" Megan asked.

"No one's told me, but if you're worried go and ask Doc Crooke or your principal, I'm sure they'll help you," Donovan suggested, "I do know that they can't read your thoughts, so Gerry's quite safe. They don't put anything in or take anything out of your brain; they just record impulses."

"Gerry's got a lot of impulses," Billy looked innocently at the reporter, "but we manage to control him!"

"There's nothing to worry about, and at least you'll be out of the classroom for a while," Donovan reassured them after the laughter. That thought seemed to brighten them, except Marcus.

"I still think that it's a waste of time!" he grumbled.

Chapter Eighteen

To prevent any speculation about their frequent meetings, they now met on the internet in conference. It was Elizabeth's idea as her appearance always drew attention, mainly because she was an outstanding beauty, and an outsider always drew attention, and she could also guarantee that the meetings were secure with the FBI network.

"How are things down there?" she asked.

"Well, the mayor's sold on it, he's spouting hot air and propaganda, but his history is way off line," Donovan told her, "he thinks everything was invented in the good old US of A."

"It isn't?" Elizabeth looked surprised, and then laughed, "I get that all the time."

"Very funny! The high school principal has doubts about the intentions and the uses behind the scheme, but he likes the idea of more information." Donovan continued, "The kids are spooked by the idea of tests, they think that we're trying to read or alter their minds, but I told them to see Crooke."

"Thanks, as though I don't have enough to do!" Crooke sighed.

"It sounds okay to me," Elizabeth leant forward and looked at some notes on her desk, "That's about the same everywhere. Where there was some doubt, we put the argument forward that it could improve the kids, and that changed things most of the time. The Californians welcomed it without question, but we won't be sending a team there."

"The only one that didn't go along with it was young Marcus, and that worries me," Donovan informed her.

"Marcus, that's the brainy one with glasses?" Elizabeth had a good memory, but just checked, "Why does that bother you?"

"Because he's brainy!" Donovan rubbed his eyes, "There's something about him that just doesn't settle with me."

"He's just a kid, what can he do?" The sheriff didn't sound worried.

"I just said that he's brainy, and he's a teenager; who knows what he'll get up to!" the reporter summed up his thoughts, "I'll remind you that teenagers are rebels!"

"I'm getting jumpy just listening to you," Crooke leant into the camera, "I know for a medical fact that his IQ is sky high, and he's probably the brightest person in the state and maybe the country."

"But he's just one kid!" the sheriff continued to protest.

"You forget that he's a member of a group of kids, and God knows what a group of rebels can do," Crooke pointed out.

"I'll keep an eye on them," the sheriff decided.

"We'll all keep an eye on them," Elizabeth corrected him, "Remember that this is a team effort."

Chapter Nineteen

To shake the cobwebs out of the students, especially the football team, Coach 'Ding-Dong' Bell had them all on the field in the first week of term. Joel was the star player and took to the training without any difficulty or complaint. Marcus, on the other hand, restricted himself to a few laps on the track. He reminded Coach of a drunken spider as he ran!

Billy hated these early sessions as he quickly got out of breath, and suffered twinges as his muscles unused for a while tried to cope with the regime. Obviously, fooling around during the holiday wasn't enough to keep his body up to scratch. On the other hand, the first game was in a couple of weeks, and he had to get up to speed before that.

It was on the Friday afternoon that three huge trucks pulled into the school and disgorged a small army of technicians, and just as the students were leaving for the weekend, they were given envelopes. The gang stood and watched them unload.

"Jeez! They're going to tear us apart!" Gerry read the enclosed letter.

"I expected as much," Marcus nodded, "They are going to take samples and scans to find out what makes us tick."

"Hey, they may even do our folks!" Joel raised his eyebrows and waved the letter, "I wonder what my old man will say about that!"

"It makes sense. We are what we are because of our parents – genes and all that," Marcus tucked the letter away.

"What if you don't wear jeans?" Gerry tried to look intelligent, and failed!

"I can't see what they hope to find," Billy grunted, "How is this going to explain why Joel is so big and you're so brainy?"

"There's even an IQ test," Gerry grumbled.

Billy cackled, "Just make sure that you spell your name right!"

"Ah, the mysteries of science!" Marcus patted Billy's shoulder, "I could explain it to you, but you'd probably fall asleep."

Billy gave a mock sigh, "You're probably right!"

Elizabeth Hanningford thought so too. She came into town the following day and was trying to explain to the sheriff what they expected. She could see that it was causing him some pain.

"It's quite simple, something is happening over a large part of the country, and we can't explain it. Your two friends gave us additional leads with their research, and we suspect that it's neurological. It's like an epidemic, but it's an unknown cause, so we have to test everyone or at least a large proportion of the population."

"But the cost must be astronomic!" the sheriff objected.

"Have you any idea of the cost if an epidemic gets out of hand? This way we get a better base to find out more. If something happens to those we have tested, we can find any changes, and that would steer us towards a solution, and we could also use the data for other things later."

"I guess you're right," the sheriff capitulated.

Donovan had a different view when they all met later, "It infringes on a person's rights!"

"It will also protect them from many things," Elizabeth retorted, "Surely their safety is more important than their civil rights!"

"She's right!" Crooke sided with her, "I hate the idea of someone invading my inner privacy, but I hate the idea of a parasite invading my body even more."

"You don't know it's a parasite or anything else," the reporter countered.

"These tests will eliminate many things, and isolate a few probable areas to investigate further, without them we are just guessing," the doctor replied.

"It's no use arguing, on Monday the tests start where we sent the teams." Elizabeth leant back, "We've already had scores of legal complaints similar to yours, but we've dealt with them, after all, we do need more intelligent and capable people to survive as a nation without the question of a biological anomaly."

"Do you think that it's a biological weapon?" Donovan looked startled.

Elizabeth looked at him through half-closed eyes, "We can't rule out anything."

Crooke thought that through, "It's very easy to use biological weapons, but so far any attempts have been rather crude and easily countered, like the anthrax attacks a few years ago. Something more subtle may be harder to detect."

"Damn it!" the sheriff looked pissed, "I thought that this was some natural thing, but now you're suggesting that someone's making war against us!"

"Keep your shirt on, it's just a possibility," Elizabeth calmed him down, "Next week we'll start to see something more concrete than suppositions."

Chapter Twenty

The first things that Billy and the gang had to suffer were multiple IQ tests in the Gym.

Gerry looked happy, "They were easy, no nuclear physics, but why five tests?"

"Each test reveals something different," Marcus answered smugly, "The brain is very complex and works in several different ways, and is also different in every individual."

"Oh right! Do you know what they were testing?" Billy asked.

"Not a clue!" Marcus didn't seem bothered by not knowing, "A lot of the result depends on the interpretation of the answers, and we wouldn't know what that will be."

"Sounds more like guessing to me!" Gerry scratched his head.

"Most of it is!" Marcus replied with an expression of having a sour taste in his mouth.

For the next tests the following day, they entered one of the trucks. Billy blinked at the bright lights and rows of machines. They took blood and urine samples and even some hair and finger-nail clippings.

"What are you looking for?" he asked of the technician.

"Anything unusual like heavy metals, that sort of thing."

"I'm a country and western man myself," Billy thought that was a clever answer.

In the next truck he was X-rayed from head to foot, and finally in the last truck he had an MRI scan of his skull and upper body. The pounding machine left him with an equally pounding headache, but they gave him a CD with the scan results. It was almost a relief to have Coach shouting at them on the field afterwards, but the torture wasn't over.

The following morning a fourth truck had joined the others, and Billy was one of the first to enter. This time they attached electrodes mainly to his skull, and then showed him a range of pictures. It was explained to him that they were just measuring the brain's reaction to stimuli.

On Friday evening they all met in the Barbed Wire Grill as normal.

"That was the weirdest time I've ever had," Gerry started the conversation.

"I thought that would have been kissing that girl with braces," Billy jibed.

"He doesn't talk about it much," Joel added his part, "I think he was tongue-tied!"

Gerry grinned and joined in their banter, "You all thought that it was a long kiss, but I was just trying to get away!"

Megan laughed with the others, "I think you're cruel to make fun of her. What was her name?"

Gerry shook his head, "I don't know as we couldn't speak!"

When the laughter subsided, they got back to the original subject.

"What do you think it's all about?" Joel's bass rumbled out of his chest.

"They're trying to classify us," Marcus said solemnly.

"Can they do that sort of thing?" Billy had a firm set to his mouth, "I thought that was what the Nazi's were doing to the Jews during the war."

"It was very common between the wars, and by many nations not just the Nazis," Marcus informed them, "Of course, they didn't have the technology that we have today, and some of the 'science' used then was laughable."

Megan shuddered, "Ugh! I saw some films about that, and they were bestial. How can anyone treat another human being like that?"

"That was the reason for the 'science'; it gave them the excuse of thinking that some of us weren't human. We did the same during slavery, so we can't be too critical," Marcus picked up his soda and gave a long pull on the straw.

"But we know better now!" Megan scowled at Marcus's bent head, "Surely they can't use what they find against us!"

"I asked one of the techs what they were looking for," Billy remembered, "and he said that they were looking for heavy metals and stuff."

"Our bodies have small amounts of everything, including metals and poisons," Marcus explained, "that's normal, but if we get too much of anything it can lead to some pretty awful things."

"Weird things," Megan had a surprised expression as a thought occurred to her, "Could this be linked to what happened here?"

"That's possible, but these tests are going on all over the country, not just here," Billy felt as though he'd missed something as he spoke.

"What if weird things are happening everywhere?" Megan's voice had shrunk to almost a whisper.

"We would have heard something, wouldn't we?" Joel looked at his companions who shrugged.

"Why should we?" Megan's small voice answered him, "It's a big world and things are happening that we never hear about."

"We have to be careful that we don't start another conspiracy theory," Marcus smiled to ease the tension, "there are too many as it is."

Billy's face cleared, "Yeah, you're right, it's too easy to make up mysteries. I guess it's just what we're told."

Megan looked at him, and it was obvious that she didn't go along with that idea, but she said nothing. Marcus said nothing but just stared a Megan.

Chapter Twenty-One

The early results of the tests started to appear, and Elizabeth read the reports at her desk. She read them three times before throwing the last down and frowning out of the window. They had included the boys, Megan and Suzy, and extended to include Suzy's parents and the other parents; nothing unusual had been found!

She had half hoped that there would be some clue that would lead somewhere. The total cost of the investigation was colossal, and if a clue could be found early enough, they could concentrate on that and reduce costs.

In the distant past, she had studied organic chemistry, and an opening in the FBI laboratories had introduced her to forensics. From then on, her career had advanced until she was a head of a department. She smiled at the thought; other departments had staff that in places could be measured in hundreds, but all she had was three, including herself.

Tracy Young was an able-bodied firearms expert that they had imported from the US Marine Corps, and the last was James Fallon, an electronics expert and a graduate of MIT. It was a strange mix, and they had been drafted together because their previous departments had been restructured, and that now there was less demand for the type of work they previously did.

Their task was to look for anything unusual that stood out from the normal run of events. Considering that there were a considerable number of murders, accidents and assaults every year that were often bizarre, finding the unusual was a major task in itself. It wasn't surprising that the other departments referred to hers as 'the X-Files' and her two companions as 'Mulder' and 'Scully'.

None of them believed in UFOs or aliens, and the only pictures on the walls were those of landscapes. Nor were they buried in the basement, but instead enjoyed a splendid view over the city of Portland, Oregon from the top floor of a modest four storey building.

Despite having a small staff, Elizabeth had all of the FBI's facilities at hand. On every desk was a video phone and a computer linked to the main computer, and a quarter of the office was occupied by printers and fax machines. There were just three filing cabinets, one for each of them, and they were virtually empty as each peculiarity was tracked down and found to be a natural occurrence, and the files sent down to records.

It was a tedious task to hunt down for causes of some bizarre event only to find that it was a natural occurrence, and that was what usually happened. This current peculiarity was at present only an anomaly, and she expected that nothing would come of it, nothing to cause alarm.

What was needed was as much data as possible, and until that was all in, it was no use guessing what lay behind it, if indeed they were connected. From what she could see so far, it was a run of almost unassociated events, but they would probably sort themselves out into several categories. On the other hand, there could be something, and that's why her department existed.

There were two lines of thought concerning the investigation if the events were linked. The first was that this was a natural cause and that would involve the Health Departments, and the second was that this was a form of terrorist attack or a fore-runner of an attack; a trial run. That would involve all of the security forces, and internationally as well.

She punched up the latest reports and read them carefully. Where they like the earlier events? Was there an obvious and alternative explanation? She sighed and rose from her chair and walked to the wall map. Finding the two locations, she placed a pin in each. The map disturbed her most as it was so obvious, a broad belt of incidents from east to west.

At first, they had thought that it, whatever 'it' was, was spread by road or rail, but there was no road or rail that followed the same path unbroken. They then thought that it might be a contaminant from an aircraft, but that proved to be a false hope.

The door opened behind her, and she turned to see Fallon holding out a coffee for her.

"Teacher's pet!" He smiled as she took the cup. The most startling thing about Fallon was his eyes; they were blue but so light that they could hardly be seen. Above that was a crop of sandy hair topping a very skinny frame. He reminded her of a matchstick.

"Some more?" he waved his coffee at the map.

Elizabeth nodded, "Where's Tracy?"

"He went off to look at one of those and said he'd be gone all day."

"I don't think he'll find anything, even if he spent the week there!" She was not angry, just disappointed at the lack of progress.

"I've had a thought about this," Fallon nodded to the map; "if they were computers, I would say that this was an upgrade."

"And the brain's a computer," Elizabeth pulled a face, "I can see your point, but the girl running off half naked was hardly an upgrade!"

"I would say that some young men would disagree with you," a mischievous smile hovered around the corners of his mouth.

"You can come with me next time and meet the young men. They were horrified and puzzled at the incident." She didn't think it was that amusing.

"I'd be glad to, but the majority of these incidents could have a simple explanation. If it weren't for that map, I wouldn't bother to find an explanation."

"Nor would I, but you're the computer expert, and it was computers that highlighted them," Elizabeth took a sip of coffee, "Have a check on the states that are not shown on the map, just to make sure that they are confined to this belt."

Chapter Twenty-Two

The aircraft duly 'crashed' in just the right area where any fallout would cover as much of the belt of incidents as possible. There were some tremendous explosions and an impressive amount of smoke and flames.

Several large convoys of army trucks had delivered a huge amount of pyrotechnics and aircraft parts, mainly an ancient Boeing B-52. There were an impressive explosion and a column of smoke reaching into the sky. Donovan was so impressed that he phoned Elizabeth to make sure that this was their staged accident.

"Yeah, it sure looks impressive!" she replied, "I had a few doubts of my own if it was our 'accident'. I did ask them to make it a real big one, but this has surprised me!"

"Well, it'll be seen for miles, and I understand that the smoke column has created an attraction for airline passengers."

"We're already getting reports of people migrating from the area, and all the nuts have come out of the woodwork saying that it's the end of the world. It seems to be working!" the agent concluded.

He went through the motions of collecting the news, including reports of several fatalities, but Elizabeth assured him that the area had been cleared. Conspiracies and false reports were starting before the news had appeared on TV!

There was the expected hue and cry about carrying dangerous cargoes over the country, and several TV programs investigated the transport of nuclear material by road and rail. As expected, the Senate called for an investigation and granted relief funds for the affected areas, just what Elizabeth wanted!

Mobile teams were rushed to the suspected contamination areas, and even had to go through the ridiculous charade of wearing Hazmat suits! Further out, more low-key units carried out safety checks.

There was a brief panic for the FBI office when someone said that the huge cloud of smoke several miles high was going in the opposite direction to the alleged contamination. It had to be explained that it was the upper atmosphere where the jet streams carried the radiation and that no attention was to be paid to the normal flow of lower altitude clouds. It was almost true!

Crooke had a lot of admissions from people saying that they were suffering from sickness. Most of them just had the 'flu, and he prescribed medicine and calmed them down.

Donovan was inundated with calls asking for the latest update, including one from the mayor if it were advisable to vacate the area. The sheriff had been correct in that their leader was not fearless! The sheriff had to deal with questions from nervous people, and he told them that they should just continue as normal and allow the emergency services to complete their task.

Crooke and Donovan met in the Grill and found it difficult to keep the laughter from their faces. If it weren't for the anxiety expressed by the citizens of White Tail Butte, it would have been impossible!

"I feel for them really," Donovan wiped away the smile with his hand, "Do you remember those films in the fifties showing how to react in a nuclear attack?"

"I don't know how old you think I am but I have seen them." Crooke looked round the Grill as he talked; he was trying to gauge public reaction.

"Waste of bloody time! All that they did was to create a feeling of paranoia," Donovan snorted, "The advice was that if you saw a flash, dive for cover, but the truth was that by the time you saw a flash it was too late!"

Crooke stopped looking around the diner, "Now they're going through it again. I'm expecting a few cases of depression and bad nerves. Look at their expressions!"

Donovan glanced quickly and saw that no one was laughing.

Chapter Twenty-Three

Bogden Sawicki swallowed the last of his breakfast coffee, kissed his wife goodbye, told his two children to be good at school and walked out to his car. He dumped his attaché case on the front passenger seat and checked the road before pulling out to drive from Orland Park to his office in downtown Chicago.

It was a normal Monday with too much traffic, but the sun was shining on the autumn leaves, and there was still some summer heat in the air. On Sunday he had taken the family into the hills and enjoyed a picnic, something they did while the weather was good, and he couldn't remember the fall colours being so vivid. In short, he was in a very good mood.

He stopped at some traffic lights and hummed an old Nat King Cole number, 'The Lazy, Hazy, Days of Summer', but then he saw something that stopped the music. Crossing the road in front of him was a lizard, no not a lizard, but a six-foot high Tyrannosaurus Rex! What was even more remarkable was as it turned to stare at him; it was wearing a fedora and carrying a brief-case.

Bogden stared at the creature with his jaw somewhere near his navel, until it cleared the road and disappeared round a building. He became aware that horns were sounding off around him and he hastily selected drive and pulled away.

He drove automatically, trying to understand what he had just seen. He thought, 'It must have been a costume, some kid having some fun. Damn good costume though; I wonder how it worked.'

He smiled at himself, at his reaction, and settled down to completing the journey, but out of the corner of his eye he saw another T. Rex loping along the sidewalk. He slowed and studied it, and decided that it was very realistic. The back legs couldn't be operated by a human leg; they bent the wrong way, so how did it operate?

Then he noticed that none of the other people on the sidewalk were even giving it a second glance. That struck him as unusual; perhaps there was something on that he hadn't heard about and they expected to see a miniature T. Rex!

'That was the only rational explanation', he thought as he pulled up at another set of traffic lights. As he waited for the other stream of traffic to pass by, he continued thinking about the strange creatures, and then he gaped. Among the cars and trucks crossing in front of him appeared a full grown Brachiosaurus that bent its long neck to pass under the light cables across the road.

'There must be an expo on somewhere!' he thought as he studied the monster. During the summer he had taken the kids to a dinosaur show, and the full-sized T. Rex and Raptors were very realistic. He knew that it took three or four operators for each dinosaur, but they didn't run; to support the huge weight of the machines, they stood on moving plates. These dinosaurs walked normally, lifting each foot clear of the ground.

Then he remembered that in Japan they had a computerised humanoid robot that walked almost normally and could even climb steps. These must be more advanced than those at the dinosaur show! He turned towards the car next to him to make some comment to his fellow commuter and froze.

Instead of seeing the sleepy and bored face of a fellow traveller, he was looking into the unblinking eye of a Triceratops. He looked down at the rest of the animal and saw that it was complete with the three horns and the large frill, just like the pictures in his son's picture book.

The absurd situation hit him, and he began to laugh uncontrollably. In his mirror, he saw a queue of giant dinosaurs were waiting patiently in the queue of cars at some traffic lights! At the sound of his laughter the Triceratops turned to look at him and flicked out a long, blue, forked tongue, and that made him laugh all the more.

A traffic cop arrived to find out what was holding up the traffic. He took a statement from the driver of the 'Triceratops', which looked to him remarkably like a standard GM pickup and trailer. He was followed by an ambulance to take Bogden away, and then a truck to tow Bogden's car away.

Chapter Twenty-Four

Officer Barry Bishop didn't expect to be standing in a desert when he started his shift that evening; in fact, he never expected that for the whole of his life!

He had been in the Rapids City Police Force for little more than a year after a short stint in the US Air Force. He had never served overseas and was glad of that; it seemed an awfully dangerous place beyond the shadows of the Black Hills!

There was excitement enough in Rapids City with its casinos and normal theft and assaults, but at least no one fired rockets at you!

He had just parked his patrol car off 38th Street and was walking around the properties there. His flashlight probed into the shadows, and then he blinked. He was standing in a desert scene, and it was broad daylight!

He whirled round to find himself under a towering cliff of red rock and nowhere could he see any buildings or his patrol car. He looked down at his flashlight and realised it was not needed in the bright sunlight, and what sunlight it was. He squinted up into a dark blue sky and saw a huge red sun, far bigger than he'd seen it before, and that must be the Moon next to it he thought, but it looked strange, brighter with no craters, and bluer than he remembered.

Barry shook his head and kicked the sand at his feet. It was sand and not the concrete he'd been standing on an instant before. He drew his pistol, mainly as a comfort and not because he saw anything to shoot at.

He walked slowly towards the cliff but realised that it was a lot further away than he thought, so he turned in a circle, pointing his pistol with both hands as he examined the scene more closely.

As far as he could see, there was just red sand and not a blade of grass or a bush or trees. In the distance he could make out a line of hills, but between him and the hills it was a flat desert. There wasn't even a dead tree stump!

Having taken in the situation, he started to ask himself what had happened, and where was he. He couldn't remember anything like this place in America, but if it wasn't where was it, and how did he get here?

He looked up at the Moon again, and couldn't see the usual face or markings; it was just a bright blue disc, and if it was where it was in relation to the Sun, it should only be a crescent. Looking away from the discs he could make out a few brilliant stars, and that was wrong! It began to dawn on him that this may not be anywhere near the Dakotas, in fact, it could be a lot further than he had ever dreamed of!

The words 'alien abduction' came to his mind, but he hadn't seen any flying saucers or little green men, or even bright lights.

"Hello!" he yelled as loud as he could.

"Who are you?" came a voice as clear as crystal, but not in his ears, more like in his head.

Barry spun round and saw nothing! "Hello!" he said more quietly, "Where are you?"

"Over here, I'm coming towards you as fast as possible."

Barry spun round again and then perceived that the sand in one area was moving, rippling towards him. His grip on the pistol tightened.

He then saw that it wasn't the sand that was moving, but several strange creatures as red as the sand, and he could only make them out when they drew closer.

They reminded him of stick insects, but he hadn't seen any of this size! They were about four foot long and walked on six long skinny legs. The nearest stopped in front of him, and he could make out a swelling at one end of the stick body that must be the head as it contained a pair of jet black eyes.

"Who are you and what are you?" the voice came again. It was gentle and held no threat as far as Barry could make out.

"M – My name is Barry, and I'm a human," he stuttered.

"Ahh, we have long wondered why there were no other creatures, just us the – people." The voice had hesitated as though trying to find the right word, "I am called Slish."

"H – How'd ya do? Where is this?"

"This is Home. Where are you from?"

"I'm from Rapids City, South Dakota," Barry thought that it must sound strange to these creatures.

"Welcome, Barry from Rapidscitysouthdakota. Is it far away?"

"I'm sure that it's a damn long way!" Barry gave a small strangled laugh.

"Why have you come here? What do you want?"

"I don't know how I got here, where ever it is! Did you bring me here?" Barry could feel sweat on his forehead and running down his back.

"Ahh, excuse me for a moment." Slish didn't have a neck and had to turn his whole body round to face his companions, about eight in total. Barry's head was filled with a high pitched buzzing.

Slish turned back, and the buzzing stopped, "You are most fortunate. You have the ability to go wherever you want."

"I just want to get home and resume my patrol!" Barry stated firmly.

"Then all you have to do is think of it, and it will happen!"

"I don't understand! How can I just think of being somewhere?" Barry retorted, but a picture of his home came unbidden into his mind.

He found himself in darkness and standing outside of his home, still with his pistol drawn. His wife called the station after she found him walking around the garden and talking to himself.

It was decided that he needed some rest and professional treatment, but no one could explain the red sand found in his shoes!

Chapter Twenty-Five

Elizabeth read the report three times before placing a pin on the map. Chicago and Rapids City were right in the middle of the belt. She returned to her desk and looked across to Fallon.

"Have we had any reports of hallucinations?"

Fallon thought for a moment before answering, "Some of them are reporting seeing things, but most of these are to do with behaviour, so there could be a connection. Why?"

"We've just got a report of a motorist in Chicago who has seen dinosaurs in the morning traffic. He wasn't drunk or doped."

Fallon smiled, "If he had been on the sauce, I would have believed he saw pink elephants, not dinosaurs. What happened to him?"

"Under observation, but he appears to be having a tough time. A police officer claims to have travelled to another planet and talked to aliens." She picked up the 'phone and checked a number.

Donovan answered after the fifth ring.

"Can you and the good doctor get over here? I've got something to show you." Elizabeth asked.

"I have a clear calendar, but I'll have to check with Crooke. What's up?"

"I'll explain when you get here," Elizabeth said, "Give me a ring to confirm you're coming."

"What's the idea?" Fallon asked, "I thought that the idea was not to reveal too much."

"These guys are different; they've been around the block a few times and know how the system works." Elizabeth smirked, "They are more trustworthy than most, and they are very competent researchers; it would be just a matter of time before they connected the dots, and I would rather they do that with us."

The 'competent researchers' arrived in Portland two days later and found Elizabeth waiting for them at the airport. Fallon was acting as her driver.

"I thought I'd save you the excitement of getting lost. Have a good trip?" She introduced Fallon.

"Great thanks," Donovan grunted as they got into the back seat of the sedan, "What's the great mystery?"

"No mystery, any more than the current one," Elizabeth turned round in the front passenger seat to talk to them, "I just wanted to show you where we were up to, and see if you could add anything."

"We could have done that from home," Crooke observed.

"I don't think that it would give the same results," she looked at him, "There's a lot more to this than meets the eye."

"You've found something new," Crooke guessed.

"Yes and no, you'll just have to be patient," and she turned to face forward without any further illumination.

Elizabeth took them to an interview room, and Fallon went to fetch the file on the latest incidents from their office.

"I'm beginning to feel as though we are suspects," Donovan said as he sat down and looked round the room.

"I'm sorry about that, or are you feeling particularly guilty about something?" Elizabeth smiled, "I just wanted you to see things in a particular order. This latest incident is weirder than the others."

Fallon arrived and gave the file to his boss, who handed it to Crooke, "I think that this is in your field more than anyone else's."

Crooke quickly read the notes, giving a snort and a laugh as he did so, then he passed it to Donovan and addressed the agents.

"You're not including this in the investigation? There could be dozens of reasons that this happened; obviously, he had a nervous breakdown."

Without being asked, Fallon shoved five more files across the table for Crooke to read. He gave the agents a puzzled look and then opened the first file. This time he didn't make any noise as he read and passed them without a word to the reporter.

In a more sombre mood, he looked directly at Elizabeth, "There still does not appear to be a direct connection. People have nervous breakdowns all the time."

"I agree with you, and that was our first reaction, especially the first one who saw aliens. We're rather used to those cases, and that may still be one of those. However, there are other clues," Elizabeth ticked off the items, "They were all sober, none had taken drugs, even prescribed medicines."

"That would make them exceptions to the rest of the population," Donovan said sarcastically, "I thought snorting coke was a national past-time!"

"That might be part of the pattern that they don't take drugs," Elizabeth nodded in agreement, "Bring the files with you," and she stood up and led the way to her office.

Donovan noticed the wall map immediately, "Are these all to do with the investigation? How many are there?"

"They are all behavioural events; abnormalities, and as of now there are over two thousands of them!" Elizabeth explained as they took seats, "At first it was just the more weird ones, but then we started going back through the records and finding others, and we're still looking. All of these happened within the last eight months."

Crooke pointed at the map, "But they're all in a band! Haven't you looked outside this area?"

"We have, and you'll notice that there are some pins on the fringes that are in a different colour, those are the ones we are not sure about."

"But why a band?" Crooke looked concerned, "If it were an epidemic, it would have spread in a circle."

"We noticed that immediately, and our first thought was it followed a road or rail network, but it doesn't."

Elizabeth walked over to the map and pointed out the features, "If 'it', whatever 'it' is, was carried by road, everywhere the car or truck stopped 'it' would spread out in a circle, as you pointed out. If it were by rail, the distances would be greater, and we would see spikes shooting all over the country and up into Canada."

"It must be an aircraft then!" Donovan suggested.

"Our next thought and none of the major airlines fly along the complete route," Elizabeth returned to her seat, "We've looked at individual companies in the air and on the ground, and none of them travel a route as consistent as this!"

"How about a space-craft or satellite?" Crooke wriggled into a comfortable position and put his chin in his hand.

"We also thought of that, and do you know how much space junk is up there?" Elizabeth pulled a face, "In total, it runs into the millions, but big stuff like a kilo or more is over twenty thousand!"

Donovan whistled, "I didn't realise it was that much! Do we have any data on those?"

Elizabeth waved her hands, "It's a bit frustrating! NASA and NORAD have precise data on all of the spacecraft that everyone has launched, but there are collisions up there, and that's where the millions come in. Every time there is a collision it produces many smaller parts that zoom off in unpredictable directions, and some of that stuff has been up there for years, bumping into other stuff!" There was a silence while that information was absorbed.

Finally, Donovan asked, "Do we have any information about the predictable junk?"

"Yes, and none of it matches this path exactly."

"It could be a bit that broke off and followed a slightly different path," the reporter surmised.

"And that leads us nowhere!" Elizabeth looked grim, "They were so eager to get up there and show how clever they were; they forgot everything else."

"What about other countries, are they reporting similar events?" Crooke asked.

"Not that we know of, and would they be bothered to tell us if there were?" Elizabeth passed a hand over the map, "We are using up a huge amount of manpower collecting samples of water, soil and air, just to see if there is something there."

"Were there any biological experiments sent into orbit?" Crooke eased forward in his chair, "I remember that some were sent up by NASA."

"We have denials from other countries, but they wouldn't tell us if they had!" Elizabeth displayed her temper by throwing herself into a chair.

"It doesn't make sense!" Donovan shook his head, "Anything dropped by a satellite, deliberately or on purpose, would hit the upper atmosphere and could circle the whole globe, and the launcher would be affected as much as anyone else. It's a Doomsday weapon!"

"Now you are beginning to see why some people are getting worried!" Elizabeth snorted.

"There are a lot of people worried about the 'plane crash'," Donovan changed subject, "I assume that the 'infected area' covers the same as this band. There are reports of people migrating to Canada and Florida by the bus load."

"We tried to keep people calm, but it was expected that some would move out, at least for a while," Fallon informed them.

"I'm not surprised!" Donovan grunted, "Mention the words hazardous materials and most people would panic!"

"I read somewhere that the Holy Joes are out in force saying that it's the end of the world!" Crooke gave a sound that was a cross between a laugh and a sigh.

Chapter Twenty-Six

'Ding-Dong' Bell stood on the side-line and bellowed at the team. He was actually proud of them as they had thrashed Newbury High's team in the first game of the season, but he didn't let on and called it a fluke. Now they were playing against the last season's cup winners, Frenton High and doing well. Hell, if they could continue like this they could be this season's winners!

He watched with a critical eye as they lined up next to Joel, and then they charged! He winced as someone flew high in the air; it was Gerry turning head-over-heels before landing heavily on his shoulders, but he hung on to the ball. Then he didn't get up, and coach wondered what the damage was as he trotted over with a medic.

He needn't have worried, as with a shake of his head Gerry staggered to his feet. The medic checked him over and pronounced him sound, and the game continued.

Joel burst out of a tackle with ease, due to his greater size and strength, and passed the ball to Gerry, who ran with it for about ten paces, and then stopped, and that slowed Joel and the rest of the team. Gerry looked around and shook his head, and a Frenton player took him down with a massive tackle.

Joel plucked the player off Gerry's back with one hand as the coach ran up to them. The team had formed a protective circle around Gerry as they realised that something was wrong. Gerry sat up with a strange expression on his face.

"What's the hell wrong with you?" Coach bellowed.

Gerry looked up at him, and then down at the ball still clutched in his hands as though he'd never seen it before. He then dropped the ball and removed his helmet, and then everyone saw the blood trickling from his ear.

"Get him to the hospital and check him out," 'Ding-Dong' bellowed at the medic, "I'll be there right after the game."

Frenton won the game, which added to the coach's bad mood as he headed for the hospital, but when he got there, Billy and the rest of the gang, including Megan, had got there first.

"What's happened?" he glared the question to Billy.

"Nothing yet coach, the doc is looking at him now, and we think they're going to X-ray him and stuff. He looked pretty groggy." Billy's concerned expression softened the coach's attitude. He knew that these guys were tight and were really worried.

"It must have been that tackle," Joel rumbled, "I was surprised that he carried on."

To take their minds off what had happened, 'Ding-Dong' ran through their play and pulled it apart to show their mistakes. He was in mid-flow when Crooke appeared.

"He's got a concussion, not surprisingly," he informed them, "his eyes are out of focus, and he didn't recognise me. He just says 'trees' all the time."

"Can we see him?" Megan asked.

"Well, you can for a short while," Crooke shook his head, "but I don't know if you will get any sense out of him. We're going to take a brain scan shortly and see if there are any problems."

"I can feel for him," Joel said, "I had that funny turn during the holiday, remember that, guys? I didn't know where the hell I was. Do you think that was caused by a tackle Doc?"

Crooke looked interested, "It could be, and perhaps you should have a check-up. When was that exactly?"

Billy answered, "It was at the beginning of the holiday, and both you and Gerry wrecked your dad's store."

"Oh, don't remind me; it took ages to sort out that mess!" Joel turned away to show that he didn't want to pursue the matter.

"What actually happened?" Crooke asked as though he had never heard about it, and they story came out of their weekend, and how Joel was confused on the return trip, and both he and Gerry messed up the hardware store.

"That was just before Suzy pulled that stunt," Megan put it into a better time frame.

"Huh, both you and Gerry had a funny turn?" Crooke looked very interested.

"Yah, it felt really weird!" Joel turned back and looked embarrassed, "I didn't recognise anything."

"You looked like you'd been drinking for a fortnight when you came into the Grill the following day!" Megan reminded them.

"We only had a couple of beers each, but it could have been off," Billy defended their position.

"And no one else has had anything similar?" Crooke looked at each face.

"I felt like ripping my clothes off and making whoopee, but Megan stopped me!" Billy's face had a mischievous grin.

"I would only have found out the truth about you!" Megan countered.

Crooke smiled at their banter, but behind the smile, he had some serious thoughts, and those thoughts he expressed to Donovan that evening.

"There's more to the boy's story than we originally knew. It would appear that they all went camping on the first weekend of the summer holidays and had a few beers. On the way home, Joel had a weird experience; he said that nothing looked familiar to him, although he's lived here all his life and it was on the outskirts of town. In the following week, both he and Gerry had the experience in the store that we already know about."

Donovan leant back in his chair and stared at the ceiling, "It fits the pattern of something neurological, as you've said all along. Did he explain anything more?"

"No, they were in a group, and he looked embarrassed, so I didn't push him, but he is coming in for a checkup, and I'll ask him then. There is more."

Donovan raised his eyebrows and returned the doctor's stare, "And that is?"

"Gerry started to come round, and he said some curious things. He kept saying 'The trees', and so I asked him what he meant, and he said that all he could see were trees and some were walking. When I asked him later, he just looked at me and said that he didn't understand the question. He'd completely forgotten it!"

"He took a nasty tackle, could that explain having hallucinations?"

"It could be, but I kept thinking of the fellow who saw dinosaurs, and the other that saw aliens. I don't want to bring in a psychiatrist; I don't fully trust them, but we need some real brain-power on this." Crooke looked unhappy with his conclusion.

"You're the most educated professional we have as far as I know; what sort of person are you thinking of?"

"Someone with a wide knowledge, a lot broader than any of us that can join the dots."

Donovan scratched his head, "I think that we should contact Elizabeth before talking outside of the circle. Perhaps they have someone that can fit the bill."

Chapter Twenty-Seven

Marcus went down with a fever. It was so serious that Crooke had him admitted to the isolation ward while he checked out its causes. For a few days, the boy was in a semi-coma, and everyone was worried that he wouldn't pull out of it.

The boys, plus Megan, came every day to see if there was an improvement, and Crooke kept giving them encouragement. The truth was that Crooke was stumped, and had no idea of why the fever and coma had arisen, and just went through the general regime to reduce the fever.

Then one morning Marcus opened his eyes and looked around him in surprise, and demanded to know why he was there. The fever had gone, and after an extra day in the hospital he was released.

Crooke asked him if he remembered anything while in a coma, but Marcus said that he experienced nothing. With a series of weekly appointments, his parents took him home, and the gang arrived there in force shortly after. Marcus's mother was worried that he would get over-tired with the boisterous youths.

"What were you doing, sleepy head?" Gerry ruffled Marcus's hair.

"I honestly don't know," Marcus smiled at them, "I just fell asleep, and then I woke up. The doc says that I'm okay now, but wants to keep an eye on me."

"You need keeping an eye on!" Billy said as they left.

Marcus resumed school the following week and appeared non-the-worse for his experience, but on Wednesday he surprised everyone, including himself.

The lesson was math, and the master, Ralph Gordon took them through the usual procedures and leaving some looking blankly at the board. Billy copied down in his notebook and kept up. Usually, by now he and Joel would be thinking of something else, but it seemed to make sense this time and to be interesting; perhaps 'Old Gordy' had found a different method of teaching.

Marcus spoke out on the calculation presented to them, something he frequently did and was encouraged to do, and then he went into a long discussion with the master which did leave everyone else wondering what was going on. It happened so often that Billy and the rest sat back and waited. Marcus got up and started scribbling on the board, and the lesson became a debate between him and Gordy. 'We could have gone for an early lunch', thought Billy.

Gordy eventually stood back and looked at the board. "Well, I'm impressed! You've obviously been studying hard." He turned to the class, "I apologise to you all as this is far beyond anything you would be required to do, in fact, it's beyond anything that I have ever done." He turned back to Marcus, "Can you remember all this and write a paper, it'll have to be checked?"

"I think I can," Marcus looked embarrassed.

Gordy took out his cell phone and took three photographs as they had covered all three boards between them, "That might help you. I'll have a word with the coach, and you can work on that instead of sports."

'Ding-Dong' would have been furious if it had been Joel, Billy or Gerry, his stars, but Marcus wasn't built for sport, so he granted the absence.

The gang all met in the Grill afterwards and pulled Marcus's leg.

"Thanks for that, I needed to catch up on some shut-eye!" Gerry said.

"What was that all about?" Joel rumbled, "I would have understood Chinese better!"

"Chinese food you're on about," Billy countered, "what was it?"

Marcus grinned sheepishly, "I'm not sure, as he was writing I began to see other possibilities, and it just growed like Topsy."

"You're an Einstein that's what you are," Gerry raised Marcus's arm, "Ladies and gentlemen, I give you a genius!"

Megan looked at Marcus and the others with a thoughtful expression but said nothing apart from adding her congratulations.

Chapter Twenty-Eight

Elizabeth did find someone to 'fit the bill', an odd ball by the name of Demetrius Palamas, a Greek Jew who seemed capable of talking intelligently about every subject under the sun.

Donovan was sorting out his next edition when he saw a short, wire-haired man looking up at the shingle. He seemed uncertain if he wanted to enter or not, so Donovan opened the door.

"Can I help you at all?"

The oddity waved his fingers nervously, "I'm looking for a Michael Donovan."

"Look no further; you've found him!" Donovan opened the door wider and waved the man in, "What can I do for you?"

"I have been sent by Agent Elizabeth Hanningford to assist you."

This was news to the reporter, so he became cautious, "What did she have to say, and help with what?"

"That you may have a problem, most certainly you have a problem that must be resolved," the man sat down on the edge of the seat and hunched forward, "My name is Demetrius Palamas."

"Well, she never said anyone was coming," Donovan reached for his 'phone, "I'll have to check with her first if you don't mind. Help yourself to the coffee."

Before he could pick up the receiver, the 'phone rang.

"Hi, Donovan, Elizabeth here. I'm sending you a nerd, a real brain-box, but a bit eccentric."

"I'm going to be psychic and tell you his name is Demetrius Palamas." Donovan was amused and liked teasing.

There was a pause, "How the hell do you know that?"

"He's just walked into my office, and I was about to check with you." Demetrius looked up from the coffee machine on hearing his name.

"Oh hell, that's just like him! I told him that we would come down to you together, but sometimes he goes off half-cocked."

Donovan chuckled, "No sweat; what can you tell me of him?"

"We've used him several times, and he's a mine of information. He has full clearance on this, but keep an eye on him as he's been known to cause a few problems in the past, nothing serious, but he just gets so absorbed in the problem to realise what he's doing."

"What's his field of expertise?"

"Everything! He's into physics, medicine, chemistry, astronomy and a touch of the occult thrown in. I'll be down in a couple of days, and until then try and keep him out of trouble."

He replaced the receiver and studied his unexpected guest, "Well, you check out, but you've jumped the gun; you should've come down with Elizabeth."

"I wanted to see the place as soon as possible," Demetrius kept rubbing his hands nervously, "It's an interesting case, and I'm always impatient; I'm sorry."

"It's no problem," Donovan stretched out his legs, "Have you any thoughts on this at all?"

"Excuse me, but I'm a little confused. What does a newspaper office have to do with the case?"

"A pure accident," Donovan had never considered the question, to him it was just news, and "We had a case that could have been very serious..."

"I know, the young girl Suzy Barr," the little Greek appeared to be calming down, now that they were talking business, "A very frightening thing, and quite embarrassing for the young lady."

Donovan laughed, "She doesn't seem to have suffered very much, so all's well."

"No, no, we must not assume that all is well!" Demetrius started screwing his hands again." This could be something quite serious that effects everyone!"

Donovan was taken aback by the vehemence of the statement, "We didn't think of it quite that way. Before you explain further, I want you to meet Doctor Crooke who is also involved, and technically a lot brighter than I am. He'll be free this evening so in the meantime, would you like a spot of early lunch?" he checked his watch, "I should say an early dinner. I didn't realise it was so late."

"It would be my pleasure. May I leave my bags here?"

Donovan escorted him over to the Barbed Wire Grill where they took a corner seat and ordered some food.

"Where are you based?" Donovan thought to fill in a few details.

Demetrius smiled, "I have a seat in Thessaloniki, in Greece. There is a fine science centre there, but I am a guest lecturer in the USA at the moment. As soon as I finish in one place, Elizabeth finds me somewhere else to lecture, but at the moment I am between engagements."

"So you've seen a lot of the country?"

"Ah yes, last year I was in New Mexico, and was successful in visiting Alamogordo where they made the atom bombs, and just now I was in New York. It's a big country!"

"Yeah, it sure is, and I haven't seen it all!" Donovan nodded, "I always thought that when I retire, I'd get me a mobile home and see the rest."

As their food arrived, the gang entered the Grill.

"Hi Donovan, how's things today?"

"Fine boys, I want you to meet a friend of mine, Demetrius Palamas from Greece."

"Wow! You're long way from home mister!" Gerry shoved out a hand, and the rest followed. Donovan watched closely and saw a flash of recognition in the Greek's eyes as each boy, and Megan was introduced.

Marcus was introduced as the genius, and that had to be explained. Obviously, that particular story had not reached Demetrius.

"You should have seen Gordy's face at the end," Billy laughed at the thought, "Now Marcus has to write it up. I think that it's a punishment for beating the master!"

"Aw shucks! It wasn't all that great!" Marcus looked down at his shoes.

"No, it's an achievement, and you should be proud," Demetrius declared, "Well done!"

"We'll leave you to it. See ya later." The gang made their way to another table.

"You recognised the names," Donovan stated after they left.

"Yes, these are among the first people that were investigated," Demetrius kept looking at them, "They appear perfectly normal."

"As far as we can tell, they are, as far as teenagers can be!"

"What do you make of the small one, Marcus?" Demetrius looked keenly at the reporter.

"I'll have to find out more about what happened in class, but he was always the bright one."

"Bright enough to outshine the teacher?" Demetrius gave the reporter a sideways glance.

Donovan thought about that one, "It's possible, but I'll contact the school before making up my mind," and he started on his meal.

"I thought you'd be here!" Crooke had entered and looked curiously at the Greek.

"Sit down and have a meal," Donovan pushed out a chair, "This is Demetrius Palamas; Elizabeth sent him."

Crooke's mouth opened in a silent 'Oh', and he sat down. He looked over to the gang and waved, "That boy seems to have recovered."

"What boy?" Donovan looked blank, "Are you referring to Gerry's bad tackle?"

"No, Marcus, he went into a coma a week ago, but seems back to normal now!" Crooke looked unconcerned and studied the menu.

Donovan slowly laid down his knife and fork, "I hadn't heard about it. We were referring to him beating a teacher at math. Why was he in a coma?"

Crooke shrugged, "No idea, he recovered too quickly for a decision to be made."

"Excuse me, Doctor, these are the boys where two have had a 'funny' incident, and now a third has had an unexplained event," Demetrius looked intensely at the doctor, "Don't you think that it raises a question?"

The waitress arrived, and Crooke ordered his meal before returning to the subject, "I was more concerned with the boy to give any thought to it, but you're right; is there a connection?"

Donovan looked over at the gang with a thoughtful expression, "He has a coma, and then produces advanced mathematics; that's weird alright!"

Crooke looked puzzled, "What's this about mathematics?" Donovan filled in the details.

Demetrius turned to Donovan, "Have comas been included in the data?"

"We haven't gone out of our way to look for them, and Elizabeth has the complete record and would know, but as far as I know, the comas were just a side issue, if at all."

"The other boys have not suffered any 'incidents'?" the Greek pushed his plate away.

"Not that we know," Crooke looked concerned, "Now you've got me worried!"

"I must ask Elizabeth to bring any data on comas when she comes here," Demetrius decided, "It appears that there may be many more events that we have not recorded."

"What is your purpose here?" Crooke asked, and Donovan answered.

"He's a general science advisor to the FBI, and Elizabeth thinks that he can see things that specialists and idiots like us cannot."

Demetrius nodded, "Just so, but you should not consider yourself so badly, and already there are aspects of this that are disturbing. Consider the case of the girl Suzy; she has no memory of what happened, only what she has been told. Would you not think that is a form of unconsciousness, a coma? The two boys were in a confused state, and that could be called a partial coma; a part of their brains was asleep."

Donovan leant back and gave the new idea some thought before replying, "The autistic boy Timmy could be considered to have been in a type of coma, and then woke up, and the old girl was certainly not all there until she woke up!"

"I would prefer the term 'a different state', such as the different states of matter," Demetrius concluded.

Crooke had started to eat his meal but paused, "I can see where you're going with this. You're saying that the brain can operate at different levels, such as a mixture of oxygen and hydrogen can exist as a solid, a liquid or a gas."

"You must not forget plasma," Demetrius smiled at the doctor's understanding.

"You're getting a bit beyond me," Donovan interrupted, "You're talking about water at different temperatures."

Crooke swallowed a mouthful, "Water at different energy levels appears in different forms, but is still functional in those different states."

"Yes, there is no such thing as temperature," Demetrius explained further, "As things become more energetic they give off energy that we refer to as temperature, but it is just an indication of the energy level."

"I don't see how that connects to our problem!" Donovan frowned.

"I think what our good friend is trying to say is that the brain can function in a similar way." Crooke paused to take some water, "In Timmy and the old girl's case their brains were operating at a low energy level, and Marcus, there was at an almost zero energy level while he was in a coma, but all changed their state very quickly. Is that right?"

"Basically that is correct," Demetrius confirmed.

"But I don't think that brains work the same way as each other," Donovan still looked puzzled.

"That is the problem," Demetrius agreed, "We have had an example given to us while we have sat here. The boy Marcus has had a coma, and before that he was brighter than average, but afterwards he appears to have increased that far beyond his previous state."

Donovan took a sip of coffee, "I don't know exactly what he's done, but the teacher was impressed enough to ask Marcus to prepare a paper."

"That could be perfectly natural," Crooke finished eating, "As you said, he was brighter than average to begin with, and it's not beyond reason that he's developed."

Demetrius nodded, "That is my point, and it is a subtle change such as water turning to ice by altering just a few degrees. A small change can make a remarkable difference. If you did not know the reason, would you think that ice and water were the same substance?"

Donovan paused and ordered coffee for everyone, "I can see that it would apply to Marcus, and by extension to most of the other cases, but I can't see the connection between those and Suzy and the bum Hamish that was killed."

"I can't see a medical connection between any of those and a guy seeing dinosaurs," Crooke added.

"There may not be a connection," Demetrius argued, "Hamish may have expired from just his life style, and Suzy may have had a sudden impulse, and perhaps the dinosaur man may be just delusional. What I am suggesting is that there may be a small change that produces the effect, but in different forms."

"Like water and ice," Donovan still didn't look convinced.

"We now have a new line of thought to investigate," Demetrius looked satisfied; "When Elizabeth brings in new data it may illuminate the culprit."

Crook didn't agree, "What you're suggesting may be too small to detect."

"Then we'll have to use a better microscope!" Demetrius smiled.

Chapter Twenty Nine

Ralph Gordon was surprised to receive the paper from Marcus so quickly, and that evening he read and re-read it, trying to find a flaw; even the best of mathematicians can make mistakes. Then he consulted a number of textbooks, checking that Marcus hadn't used plagiarism. During the following days, he carried it in his briefcase and read it at every opportunity. He checked on the internet and found he was going even further than he expected.

He wasn't upset that a young boy had publicly humiliated him, far from it; he was excited that he had discovered a mathematical genius.

Eventually, the principal noticed that Gordy was preoccupied in the corner of the staff room and asked what the paper was, and Gordy laid out Marcus's paper and his suggestion.

"This is totally unexpected; he has surpassed me almost overnight. Last year I would have expected that he would become a top accountant or banker at the most, but this has the hallmarks of a top mathematician in the league of Einstein or any other top physicist."

Hugh Pritchard, the Principal of White Tail Butte High, looked briefly at the paper, and then sat back to look at the master.

"Don't get me wrong Gordy, this means immense prestige to the school, but what you're saying is unbelievable. Don't you think that you're exaggerating just a little?"

"Not really, I've checked it several times over the last week, and I can't find a flaw. It's not anything new, but I can't understand how he reached this level, and his approach is novel. It's the promise that this brings; the boy needs to be better educated than this school, or I can provide."

"I'm no mathematician; just about balance my cheque book, so I'll have to take your word that this is exceptional. What do you suggest?" Pritchard asked.

Gordy took a deep breath, "I want to send it to a friend at Harvard and let the real mathematicians look it over."

Pritchard didn't seem surprised and thought only a brief moment before consenting, "We can get some publicity for the school over this, and if it is as good as you suggest, it could mean upgrading the school. Go ahead and let me know what happens. I'll contact the local newspaper guy, what's his name, Donovan, and see if he would print something."

Chapter Thirty

"What do you think is going on?" Megan and Billy were without the others for a change, and Megan posed the question. Her excuse was that she had to do a project study on some woodland and asked Billy to accompany her. She felt nervous without familiar people in lonely places, and especially the forest after the recent events.

Billy's mind must have been elsewhere, "Nothing that I can think of."

"I'm talking about the boys. First, it was Joel, and then Gerry, and now Marcus, and I'm wondering if you're going to do something odd." Megan gave him an accusing stare.

"Wait until we get into the woods, and I'll see what I can manage!" He pulled off the road next to the planned project area and stopped more suddenly than he planned. Megan had hit him hard on the shoulder.

"I'm being serious! Our friends are in some trouble, and all you can do is make jokes!" she banged the door shut.

Billy climbed out of the pickup and rubbed his shoulder, "I'm sorry, but I can't see why you're so upset. The boys are okay, in fact as far as Marcus is concerned, he's better than okay!"

"But why? Why is this happening, and why to just us?" Megan hoisted her camera over one shoulder and clutched a notebook in her other hand.

Billy shrugged his shoulders and lifted a large bag out of the pickup, "Just lucky I guess. I don't see what the problem is."

"Do you think that Joel and Gerry mucked up the store just for fun?" she was glaring at him all the time, "Did Marcus have a near death something just for fun?"

"If you put it like that, I guess they didn't, but I think it's just one of those things in life."

"Have you forgotten about Suzy or that old bum Hamish that they found dead?" Megan led the way into the undergrowth, "I tell you that something is happening here, and I'm worried that it's going to happen to all of us!"

Billy stopped in his tracks. "Why should it happen to all of us?"

"Because it's happening to us one by one." Megan pointed out.

"Now you're making me feel nervous!" Billy gave a genuine shudder.

"Good! You might have reason to be." Megan had reached an open glade where she would record her findings.

"I don't see that because something happened to some of us that it would happen to us all, that's not logical."

"I know it sounds crazy, but I feel that it's going to happen." She reached for her bag and looked around the glade.

"Oh, feelings, that's different," he said offhandedly.

"What do you mean by that?" she whirled on to him, "Are you saying that I'm a stupid, emotional female?"

Billy backed away, "No not really, but girls do feel things differently!"

"We are also good at thinking differently than stupid jocks!" She faced him with her hands on her hips.

Billy held his hands up to ward her off, "Let's not get too worked up about this. Shall we start again? You're worried that something is happening that's making us do weird things, and I can agree about the weirdness. Why should it affect everyone, and what is it?"

"Think of Marcus; did you ever think that he would better Gordy?" She poked a finger in his chest.

"Well, he's a damn sight better at math then any of us!" Billy admitted.

"I wasn't there, but how far did you understand what was going on?"

Billy threw his hands up, "Hell, it was way over my head, I didn't understand a thing!"

"Think, try to remember when it was that you lost track during a lesson, and compare that to last year. Was there a difference?" Megan poked him in the chest. Billy thought that she looked terrific!

"Yeah, I seemed to follow the logic of what they were saying, but I couldn't describe what I understood."

"And last year?" She prodded him again.

Billy grudgingly nodded, "I understood more than I did six months ago, but I'm older!"

"But you haven't been studying math during the six months, so where did all that understanding come from?" Megan cocked a questioning eye.

Billy was struck into silence. He had no answer, and he couldn't explain why what happened, happened.

Megan took a ball of twine out of her bag and some pegs, "Help me mark out the ground in meter squares."

Billy remained quiet for the rest of the afternoon, including the drive home. He was thinking hard and feeling uncomfortable at some of the conclusions that Megan had produced.

Chapter Thirty-One

Elizabeth brought twenty CDs with her and placed them on Donovan's desk. He picked them up.

"I thought that you would bring stacks of boxes. Is this all the data?"

"If I'd turned up with boxes, it would have been obvious that something was up and tongues would have wagged. Anyhow, this is a new age, and we've dispensed with paper, or haven't you heard? You'll need this one as well as they're all encrypted," she drew out another CD from her pocket. "It's all we have at present, but I've concentrated on the comas that Demetrius asked for. Where is he?"

"With Crooke. They've formed a friendship, or possibly they speak the same nerd language." Donovan smiled.

"Greek?" Elizabeth smiled at her joke.

"Very funny! They're talking about bugs and viruses."

"You've heard about our local genius?" Donovan showed her the latest headline about Marcus.

"Yeah, what do you make of it?" Elizabeth read the whole article.

Donovan shrugged, "He was always the most intelligent of the group, so I suppose it's natural that he would have got there eventually."

"But the others don't agree?" Elizabeth pulled a chair up to the desk and sat down.

"They started spouting things like development statistics, or at least Demetrius was. It would seem that Genius Marcus is off the charts."

"Don't under-estimate Demetrius, he's one of the sharpest minds we know of, and if he says it's off the charts, it is. Now, as a reward for bringing this, you can take me to dinner."

Donovan smiled and rose from his chair, "I'll lock this away first, and then I'll be delighted with your company."

The gang were all there as Elizabeth and Donovan entered the Grill, and an exchange of greetings passed between them as Donovan politely seated the agent.

"Donovan's got a girlfriend," Megan observed.

"Good for him!" Gerry gazed at the couple, "She's a looker too!"

"Down boy, she's a bit beyond school age!" Joel advised.

"I don't think she is a girlfriend," Billy corrected them, "I saw her when we had those tests, just briefly in a side office."

"I've seen her walking around town some months ago," Megan said.

"Well, that's probably when they met," Gerry wasn't put off.

"Well, it's not our business," Joel slapped Gerry's arm, "So stop staring!"

"Do you think Donovan's good looking Megan?" Marcus asked.

"If you like older men," Megan said as she pulled Gerry's head round.

"We're all older than you," Billy pointed out with a sound of hope in his voice.

"You don't act like it!" Megan looked thoughtful, and her remark was an automatic response.

"I'm beginning to appreciate older women," Gerry sighed and looked over at the agent.

"Well the next time I hear of a granny who's available, I'll let you know," Marcus said, and everyone burst out laughing.

"Megan was saying something to me this afternoon, and now we have the mysterious and beautiful stranger in our midst," Billy said when the laughter subsided, "You tell them what you said."

Megan looked a bit uncomfortable and shot Billy a glare, "I was saying that it's strange that things have happened to us, as a group. Marcus was the most extreme, and then Suzy, and then you two really fouled up the store. I wondered if things will happen to all of us, and when I questioned Billy, it would appear that something has happened to him, but very slightly."

Marcus looked sharply at her, "If it's any comfort, which I'm sure it isn't, I've had the same thoughts."

"So Billy's going to become a genius! No, I'm sure it's a god!" Gerry laughed lightly.

"We've found the God Particle!" Joel rumbled.

"The God Particle is to do with mass..." Marcus started a long explanation.

"If that's the case, I must be God-like!" Joel gave a rumbling laugh.

"The God Particle has nothing to do with God," Marcus tried to continue, "Mass causes gravity, but we don't know why things have mass, so we can't figure out gravity. Einstein ..."

"His hero!" Gerry interrupted.

"...Einstein and others since have been trying to work out a unified theory, called TOE, the Theory of Everything..."

"They're trying to find their toes?" Gerry continued baiting him.

"...and the God Particle, correctly known as the Higgs Boson is what will solve the problem. It has nothing to do with what has been happening here with us!" Marcus finished triumphantly.

"So where do my toes come in?" Gerry couldn't resist a last comment.

"You guys are impossible!" Marcus wailed, "It doesn't take much to be a genius compared to you lot!"

"We still have to find a theory of the beautiful stranger," Megan reminded them.

"I think she's a goddess!" Gerry sighed again.

"It could be coincidence, but when I first saw her she was coming out of the sheriff's office," Megan ignored Gerry's antics.

"Didn't we see Doc, Donovan and the sheriff have a serious talk back then?" Billy whispered.

"Yeah, but it still doesn't prove anything." Megan returned the whisper.

"I think I can find out," Billy said.

"How?"

Billy touched his nose with his finger and just winked.

Chapter Thirty-Two

Billy had to forego his adventure, for events overtook his plans.

A well-known Mexican criminal Tomas Ramirez had held up an all-night petrol station near Medford, killing two attendants in the process, and was suspected of heading their way. An alert was put out warning the town folk to report suspicious strangers and to keep everything locked and secure.

Sheriff Dave Reynolds and his deputies put in long hours searching out of the way places, lonely homesteads and caravan parks. Usually, they used their patrol cars but had at times had to use horses to search the forest trails where a 4x4 couldn't go.

Donovan spent a lot of time on the case, either in the sheriff's office or in the patrol car, and Billy was forced to shelve his plans.

The sheriff didn't think they would find anything, as this had happened before and the culprit usually went as fast and as far as possible, passing briefly through the district. It was to his surprise and satisfaction that the murderer was found or at least parts of him.

It was while on horseback that the sheriff saw the glimmer of metal deep in the woods, and after cautiously approaching the metallic glint on foot, it proved to be the vehicle that the murderer had stolen during the robbery.

There was no sign of Ramirez, and so the sheriff called in his deputies, and they searched far and wide. The driver's window was smashed with traces of blood on the inside and outside of the door. It didn't look like a gunshot to the sheriff, and he wondered what had caused it and whose blood was shed. Forensics would tell him that, but he didn't want to call them in until the murderer was found.

It was the youngest deputy, Andy who found the first signs; it was a human arm that had been torn away in a frenzied attack. When the sheriff saw it, he remarked on just what had done it. "It must have been a bear; no human could have done that!"

"But it's just been pulled out," Andy had recovered from a fit of vomiting; "There are no teeth or claw marks!"

The sheriff looked back to where the vehicle stood, "He was heavily armed, and could have shot a bear easily. Keep looking Andy, and if you see any signs of animals or weapons, let me know."

There was a trail of blood that the sheriff followed and led to a devastating scene; it was the decapitated trunk of a male without arms or legs either. The sheriff was glad that he'd sent Andy in the other direction. By the side of the body lay a .44 Magnum, and when the sheriff examined it, all six chambers had been fired. 'But at what?' he thought, 'there should be some signs of someone or something else'.

Andy called out, and when the sheriff got to him, he was holding up an automatic AK47 rifle. On examination, it too had been emptied at something.

"Where did you find it?" he asked and Andy pointed at some bushes off to one side. It was obvious that the Ramirez had fired the whole magazine at something, and then thrown the rifle away, and then continued running only to stop and empty the revolver before being ripped to pieces.

He decided then to call in forensics, but stayed to give protection to the team against something that seemed to come out of hell! Donovan, Crooke and Elizabeth turned up with them.

"What the hell did this?" Donovan covered his mouth with a hand.

Crooke bent over the trunk and gave it a cursory glance, "I can confirm that he's dead, but don't ask what did this!"

Elizabeth walked to where she could see as much of the scene as possible and turned round studying the angles, "This reminds me of a gang killing with several participants."

"Well I can say that there are no signs of anyone else being here," the sheriff told her, "I will agree that this looks like frenzy."

"Or another weird event!" Donovan said, and everyone turned to look at him.

Chapter Thirty-Two

The news of the killing had spread like wildfire, and when the sheriff returned with Elizabeth, Donovan and Crooke in tow, there was a large crowd gathered in front of his office. The only person who answered their questions was Donovan with a curt "Read it in the paper!"

They each took a coffee and sat down, saying nothing, but deep in their thoughts. Donovan took a cigarette from Elizabeth and broke his five-year record of abstinence. The head of the corpse had been found about a hundred feet further on, as though it had been thrown like a football.

"Where's that Greek guy?" the sheriff asked.

"Demetrius? Buried in my computer," Donovan replied.

"Is this one of the weird things that have been happening?" the sheriff asked Elizabeth.

She knew that the sheriff had been left out of the loop, but it looked as though he should be brought in, "It certainly looks weird enough!" then she turned to Crooke, "Was he torn apart?"

"It looks that way, but I'll find better evidence during the post mortem; I'll be able to see where stress has been applied."

"That would take enormous strength!" she said as much to herself as the others.

"In ancient times, they had to use horses, one for each limb," Donovan confirmed.

146

"I didn't see any horses out there, except the one I was riding!" the sheriff snorted.

"What are we looking for?" Elizabeth gave a visible shudder. Obviously, she had thought of something.

"And does it fit in with the rest of the odd things?" Donovan added.

"What gets me is that the creep emptied an assault rifle and a .44 Magnum, and there would have been signs of the battle at least, but I would have expected another body, parts or blood, but not necessarily human." The sheriff threw his hat on the desk.

"Wait until I've completed the PM and perhaps there's another answer," Crooke stood, "I've had a long day and still have to check in at the hospital. I'll see you tomorrow."

"If this is an 'event', it's a serious one, and I have to tell you that there is more," Elizabeth looked grimly at the sheriff.

"You've been holding back! Why didn't you tell me?" the sheriff scowled at the agent, and then at the other two.

"Nearly all is outside of your jurisdiction, and mostly just odd things that do not concern any law department; just curiosities," Elizabeth informed him, "Relax, I was just saving you extra work, but this changes everything."

"It sure does!" the sheriff sat on the corner of his desk and folded his arms, "Well, let's have it!"

"So far we have thought that this was something neurological, but this is something physical, physical enough to tear someone to pieces. It's something new," Elizabeth paused, "except for Old Hamish."

Elizabeth continued by filling in a short version of what they had been investigating that produced a slack-jawed expression on the lawman's face. She finished with, "If you want to see all the 'events', that's what Demetrius is looking at now, and you can peer over his shoulder."

The sheriff shook his head, "Nah, you're right; it's not police work, but I would like to know about serious 'events' as you call them."

"You will be!" Elizabeth stood up, "There's nothing else to be done for now, so I'm off to bed."

"Let me escort you back to the motel," Donovan stood and waited for the answer.

"How gallant! Thank you and G'night sheriff." Elizabeth took the reporter's arm.

As they left the office, they 'accidentally' ran into Billy. He had seen Donovan and the agent enter the sheriff's office, and he'd hung around for them to emerge.

"Hi Donovan, a nasty business I hear," he spoke to the reporter but was looking at the agent.

"Hi Billy, you'll have to wait for the official version." Donovan was amused at seeing him and suspected that the boy had been waiting.

"I know that, I was wondering who your pretty friend was."

Donovan sighed and looked at Elizabeth who stretched out her hand. "Special Agent Elizabeth Hanningford, FBI."

The admission surprised Billy, "Golly, are you here about this murderer?"

"I am now!" She also had an idea what Billy was doing.

"I saw you a couple of months back, so this isn't the first time you're in town. Do we have a Russian spy here?" Billy half-joked.

Elizabeth gave a throaty chuckle, "Very observant of you, but I'm not allowed to comment on ongoing investigations."

"Aw, that's just what they say in the movies. I won't keep you, but it was nice to meet you, and I hope you stay a while."

"Billy, don't broadcast that the FBI are here," Donovan said seriously, "It'll only stir up a lot of gossip."

"Oh sure, I understand. Goodnight!"

Billy's original idea was to interrogate Donovan by himself, but to his surprise, the agent made it much easier, although he felt as though he had been the one interrogated.

Chapter Thirty-Three

"It was dead easy!" he told the others the following day, "She didn't deny anything, but she didn't say why she was here a few months ago."

"Well she wouldn't, would she?" Megan snorted, "I still think that there is something happening that we're not being told about."

"Have you heard what happened to that Mexican guy? Ripped to pieces I've heard!" Gerry said ghoulishly and smacked his lips.

"That's what we like about you Gerry; you're not violent and bloodthirsty!" Billy punched Gerry's shoulder and hoisted his bag over the other shoulder. They were off to class where they were looking forward to Marcus making another scene.

"I'll see you guys later," Megan walked off to her class.

"This isn't right!" Marcus grumbled.

"Going to class, or Megan leaving?" Billy looked at his skinny friend.

"Who did you say went into the sheriff's office?" Marcus asked.

"Well, there was the sheriff obviously, FBI, Crooke and Donovan."

"Two cops, a medic and a reporter," Marcus pushed his glasses higher on his nose, "That sounds like a strange mix, and the FBI and reporter are very friendly!"

"She is very nice and better looking close up," Billy said, "I wish I were Donovan!" and he let out a sigh.

"I'm not referring to Donovan's love life," Marcus sounded exasperated, "What do they all have in common and won't tell anyone?"

"Dunno! What's the answer?" Gerry grabbed Billy's arm, "Did you tell her that she's a goddess?"

"This isn't a quiz, you moron!" Marcus snapped, "And she's far too old for you."

"Ah, but I can look from afar!" Gerry assumed the expression of a love sick puppy.

"I know what this reminds me of," Billy slapped Gerry's shoulder, "it's like one of those things that Gordy puts on the board and leaves a bit off, and then waits for us to find out."

"Well done young grasshopper; that's exactly what it is," Marcus beamed at him, "You've been paying attention!"

"I have to you and Billy; she's gorgeous!" Gerry had a satisfied gleam in his eye.

"Can we raise our thoughts a little higher?" Marcus snapped again.

"It's in my heart!" Gerry said.

"I think it's a lot lower," Marcus shook his head in mock disbelief, "We are missing some information, and we have no idea what it is or where to look."

"I can ask the pretty FBI lady!" Gerry offered.

"She'd chew you up!" Joel gave a rumbling laugh.

"We'll continue this later, and in the meantime, someone can give Gerry a bromide!" Marcus led the way into the classroom.

Chapter Thirty-Four

The gang met at the Grill after school, and the discussion they had was almost a mirror of one earlier in Donovan's office.

"There's something going on, and it's frightening me!" Megan crossed her arms in a defensive posture, "That's the wrong word, disturbing would be better!"

"I've been thinking the same thing," Marcus said, "What happened to Joel and Gerry was almost comical, and Suzy was slightly more serious. Old Hamish was sad but could be explained by the booze he drank. What happened to me also has a comical element, and all these things can be explained away as from natural causes. This latest, if we are to believe the scuttlebutt, is far more serious, more violent."

"It would seem that it's escalating from the comic to the diabolical!" Megan shuddered.

"Exactly, it's a progression;" Marcus held up a finger, "what we don't know is who, what, and why."

"I can answer the 'who'," Billy answered, "There was no one else involved with Joel, Gerry or you; it was nobody!"

"Then that leaves 'what'," Marcus liked to bounce his thoughts off his friends, for despite what he said, they were not morons.

Joel proved that, if it was something, and we were not aware of it, it must be invisible."

"And what is it that is invisible, but all around us?" Marcus prompted.

"Microbes, but I've never heard of one that can have different effects to different people," Megan still hugged herself.

"What are those effects?" Marcus didn't wait for an answer and continued, "Joel and Gerry were confused, I became super-smart, Suzy went nuts, Hamish died, the murderer was torn apart. What else do we know?"

"There is a kind of connection there," Billy wagged his finger, "The FBI are chatting to a reporter, the sheriff and most importantly, the doc. It could be something medical!"

"Well done my acolyte!" Marcus took off his glasses and polished them on his shirt-tail, "It's easy to see why the sheriff is involved, but why the reporter? As far as I know, Donovan has no medical degrees or police experience."

"He is nosey!" Joel offered, "He ferrets around all day."

"That's what they all do," Megan looked up for the first time, "He finds stories, the sheriff and FBI solve crimes, and Crooke deals with medical information."

"Precisely! There is some information that all have received!" Marcus said triumphantly, "Now all we have to find out is what that can be!"

"What about the 'why'?" Gerry asked.

"Finding out 'what' will probably give us that answer," Megan concluded.

"I'm wondering if this is something like germ warfare!" Marcus said.

"You're not serious?" Joel rumbled, "You think that someone's attacking us with microbes?"

"It's something that I was considering," Megan admitted, "that or chemicals."

That put a stop to their conversation as each examined their inner thoughts and fears.

That was the same question raised later in Donovan's office.

"We've had the results back from the labs at Quantico," Elizabeth told them, "They were tested for every type of material that we know of, and it came up blank!"

"This was on all of the victims, the boys, the old lady and Timmy the autistic boy?" Crooke tried to be precise.

"All of the victims, right across the country!" Donovan looked surprised. He thought that something would have been found on at least one person. "There were no abnormalities at all?"

"Just what you would expect in the average person," Elizabeth folded her arms, "Where do we go from here?"

"I find that result as abnormal," Donovan said.

"How come?" the sheriff asked.

"I think I know what Donovan means," Crooke replied, "There are thousands of cases from all walks of life over a large part of the country, but not one has taken drugs or is on medication, or of a need of it. It's totally unusual for such a sample to be so healthy! Were there any pregnancies?"

Elizabeth nodded, "A hundred or so, but everything checked out as normal."

Demetrius spoke from the corner of the room, "You are correct in your assessment; it is almost unknown for statistics to show such a result. In that, we have our first clue!"

"That's a clue?" the sheriff raised his eyebrows, "We won't get anything with such a weak case!"

"It may not hold up in a law court, but it's a direction that we must look," Crooke raised his hands, "It's so unusual that I don't know where to start; I usually deal with unhealthy people."

"That Billy was a bit inquisitive the other night," Donovan changed tack.

"It's a small town, and people are always curious," the sheriff explained.

"It's a good job we found the Tomas Ramirez here," Elizabeth smiled at Donovan, "at least I could be honest and have a reason to be here."

"Ah, but he remembered you we here earlier, and that could cause a problem," Donovan pulled his lower lip, "I can imagine that they are discussing that and making up all sorts of stories."

"He seemed to think that we were romantically involved; that should satisfy them if no one else." Elizabeth's smile broadened as Donovan's face went pink.

"That's all very well, but where do we go from here?" the sheriff thumped his desk, "As far as I can see that apart from possibly Tomas Ramirez, there's been no crimes, and I can't move until there is one."

"There are two places we can investigate," Demetrius took the lead, "The first is to catalogue all of the similarities from the tests, and the second is to find out what they were doing just before the event."

"My bosses are already asking when this will finish," Elizabeth frowned, "Now I have to ask for another search. This isn't going to be fun!"

"Is there anything we can do?" Crooke looked at the others, "Our time won't show up on your records."

"There is an enormous amount of data to sift through, and that will take computer time," Demetrius explained, "I can do the initial correlation here, and if I can use the FBI's wonderful computer afterwards, I can quickly gather results."

"What about their activities before the events?" Donovan asked.

"There's no record of that, and I'm afraid it's going to be face to face interviews," Elizabeth sighed.

"Not really," Donovan brightened up, "A lot of my story search is done on the telephone, fax or e-mail. I can send out some e-mails to the victims, and those that don't have a computer, I can telephone."

Elizabeth thought that over, "It should cover most of the cases if not all, but you'll have to be an official agent; they may not reply to a journalist, and you'd better get a good excuse to contact them."

"Do I get a shield and a gun?" Donovan's smile went from ear to ear.

"Just an official e-mail address, G-man!" and for the first time they'd known her, she giggled.

Chapter Thirty-Five

Marianne Deveraux swore like a seaman, and John Deveraux blinked as he heard his wife utter the words and felt her hand crush his.

"You bastard! You did this to me! The next time you want to play with your cock, you can do it by yourself!" she said through gritted teeth.

The sister by his side smiled and tried to ease the discomfort of her patient and the spouse, "Nearly all expectant mothers go through this. Take no notice as it eases the pain."

Quite simply, Marianne was in labour.

"But we're devout Christians, and she never swears," protested the nearly father-to-be.

"If the Holy Father hit his own thumb with a hammer, I'm sure he would have a few choice words," the sister said, "There's nothing wrong with a curse at the right time, and believe me, and this is the right time!"

"You stupid, ignorant bastard!" Marianne screamed as another bolt of pain shot through her body, and John smiled uncomfortably.

"I can see the head now," said the midwife at the other end of the bed, "Just a bit more and it'll all be over."

"Fuck!" Screamed Marianne.

"No dear, you've already done that, and that's why you're here," the sister said, and despite her predicament, Marianne started laughing. It helped, and in a sudden rush, the baby appeared.

"It's a lovely, perfect little boy," the midwife announced, "Oh, that's odd!"

Marianne panicked, "What's wrong?"

"Nothing my dear, just something I hadn't seen before. He's perfect in every way."

Marianne squeezed her husband's hand gently this time, "Oh, can I see him?"

"We'll just clean him up and weigh him first." The auxiliaries removed the birth material and made things tidy as the infant was carried away. Instead of the usual crying, it was giving out a gurgling laugh.

The sister followed the midwife and whispered, "What's wrong?"

"Nothing I think, it was that the umbilical cord had severed itself without any loss of blood before the birth. Everything else if fine."

Marianne took the baby in her arms and smiled up at John, "He is lovely, thank you, my love," and then she screamed! John's face went white, and everyone froze for an instant.

The baby had opened his eyes, and Marianne thought that she was falling into a dark pool. Vertigo had gripped her, and the world spun around, and lights flashed in her mind. She nearly dropped the child, but John grabbed it before it fell to the floor.

The sister rushed over and immediately took Marianne's pulse, "What's wrong my dear?"

"I feel dizzy and sick," and to prove it, she leant over and vomited.

"You've been through an ordeal my love," said the sister, "You're bound to feel weak and a bit off for a few hours. I'll get you some glucose, and you just rest."

John offered the infant to Marianne, but she just went whiter in the face and turned her head away.

John looked at his son in confusion. He could see nothing amiss, and he was disturbed by his wife's reaction. He reasoned that it was something that would pass in a short while, but it didn't.

The team did eventually receive a report on this, but more disturbing was the eleven other births with similar stories.

Chapter Thirty-Six

Donovan sifted through the reports by the computer, "The more we get of these, the more it becomes confusing."

Demetrius paused from his typing and looked up at the reporter, "Do you know what a Bell graph is?"

"Yeah, it's to do with mean averages."

"Very good, my friend, and what do you think is the most important thing to get an accurate figure?"

Donovan paused for a moment, "A lot of data," and he smiled, "I get the point. The more data we have, the more likely we are to find a common factor."

"Several factors to be accurate," Demetrius started typing again, "The main factor may not be the one we are looking for but it might be the second or third most important factor, and that narrows down the field, we can then compare them to other data that you are gathering."

"That might be a problem as I haven't had any replies as yet." He was referring to the e-mails he had sent out.

"You must learn patience," Demetrius said, "In Greece, we know what time is."

"Yeah, you've been around for most of it!"

Demetrius just chuckled as he bent over the keyboard. He had taken over Donovan's desk and office, and the reporter was using the secretary's desk, a remnant from when he had a secretary.

Crooke burst in, "Have you seen the latest reports?"

"No, we haven't, but why the panic?" Donovan reached for the reports, but the doctor clung to them.

"It's not panic; it's excitement!" Crooke thumbed open a folder, "This woman gave birth to a healthy boy, but during the process, it was found that the umbilical cord had separated before birth."

"We're not medics, but I thought that it had to be cut," Donovan said.

"It usually is, but it's not necessary as it separates automatically a few minutes after birth, up to about twenty minutes or so. There is no record of a normal birth where it has separated just before birth."

"I thought that it was to maintain a flow of nutrients to the baby until it can cope on its own." Donovan was only mildly interested.

"That's it exactly, but this means that the baby was fully independent while still in the womb. That's impossible!"

"Are you saying that it was breathing and wide awake before birth?" Donovan asked.

Crooke's head nearly came off as he nodded, "But there's more; when the mother was presented with her new-born child, she had a screaming fit and had had nothing to do with it since. She said that she felt as though she was drowning and she saw lights. Every one of these births are virtually the same!" He then slammed the files into Donovan's hands.

Donovan stared first at the files and then back to the doctor, his jaw off latch. Demetrius carefully took the files from the reporter's hands and started reading them.

"It's another weird experience, and it has been duplicated right across the belt, from sea to shining sea!" Crooke was gasping in a funny sort of laughter, so Donovan sat him down.

Demetrius looked up from the files, "This is indeed a departure. Up until now we were investigating events that appeared to be mostly psychological in nature, but now we have physical anomalies, and they are repeated almost to the letter."

"How serious is this early cord separation?" Donovan asked.

"Ah, childbirth is not a completely simple process, everyone has its differences." Crooke had regained his composure, "Sometimes the cord can hang on for a while longer, and the child does not seem to suffer, in fact, there is some evidence that cutting the cord too early deprives the child from some vital elements from the mother. I will have to examine the babies to make a definitive decision, and then keep an eye on their progress."

"What about this 'drowning' and lights, surely that's psychological?" Donovan continued asking.

"Yes it is, but it can be caused by the stress of the childbirth and the general health of the mother. It is usually at the limit of the mother's capabilities, and that can cause some odd behaviour, including a rejection of the child." Crooke gained his composure.

"The unusual thing here is that there are almost identical cases," Demetrius added, "even to the drowning and lights, and we must not forget that these have happened in the belt of events."

"I have to get out there!" Crooke exclaimed, "I wonder if Elizabeth can help in making it official."

"I think that she can do anything," Donovan said and lifted the telephone receiver.

Chapter Thirty-Seven

Elizabeth went with him to Ketchum, Idaho, to meet Marianne and John Deveraux, and the baby that had now been named Philip.

They landed at the Friedman Memorial Airport and took a hire-car to St Luke's Wood River Medical Centre where the family were waiting for them.

Crooke first read all of the medical notes, and then talked to the midwife and sister.

"It was so shocking and sad." said the sister, "Before the birth, Mrs Deveraux was really happy and looking forward to having the child, and immediately afterwards she was the picture of a doting mother, but as soon as she held him, she became violently ill, and since then she hasn't touched the poor thing."

"I've never heard anyone scream like that before," the midwife added, "It made my hair stand on end!"

"What about the umbilical cord?" Crooke asked the midwife.

"That was strange; I'd never seen that happen before. The cord had sealed and separated all by itself, and there was no loss of fluids."

"Has anyone tried to council her?" Crooke asked.

"Oh yes, we have a psychiatrist who tried to find out what was going on," the sister replied, "It's a Doctor Jones who would be happy to talk to you; I think he's puzzled."

"Well, I think that it's time to talk to the mother and see the little boy," Crooke stood up.

"They're in separate rooms Doctor," the sister led the way, "She can't abide being in the same room – poor mite!"

Crooke had little joy with Marianne, and John sat in the corner looking frustrated and bewildered at his wife's behaviour. She said almost nothing to explain her reasons for rejecting the child and was reticent to talk about her experience, so Crooke went to look at baby Philip.

"He looks normal to me!" Crooke tickled the baby who gurgled with laughter. He bent over to examine the navel and was surprised to see that it was almost invisible. He said nothing about the observation and looked at Elizabeth.

"The baby is acting normally, but the mother has a severe case of revulsion."

"Is that unusual?" Elizabeth asked.

"It's not unknown, but almost always there is another reason behind it," Crooke looked thoughtful as he continued to play, "One reason is an abusive husband, but you can see that in this case he's devastated."

"They're very religious, and he was shocked when she started swearing!" the sister informed them, "You can't escape bad language; it's on the TV all the time now."

Elizabeth moved towards the cot, "The report said that it started when she held the baby," and she stooped and lifted the child, looking closely into his face and cooing, "How are you, little man?"

Suddenly she staggered and bent over the cot; the sister was close enough to take the baby while Crooke rushed to see to Elizabeth.

"What's wrong?" He grasped her shoulders.

Elizabeth almost collapsed in his arms, "Oh my God, it was just as in the report! It was just like falling into a dark pool, and lights were whirling round; I had the sensation of falling!"

"Sit down and breathe deeply," Crooke was alarmed; what could be happening? "I saw you eat just a couple of hours ago, so your sugar should be okay. Do you often have these spells?"

Her face was white and sweaty, "If I did they would throw be out of the firm!"

Crooke took her pulse; it was rapid and faint, "Can we get some orange juice or sweet tea?" he asked the sister. She was back in seconds with a glass of orange.

Slowly, Elizabeth's breathing slowed down, and her colour returned. Crooke looked at her and then at the baby, and then carefully lifted the child and looked closely at his face. The baby smiled back at him and gurgled.

Crooke felt nothing, but he thought that the child should be changed, judging by the aroma. He looked once more at the recovering agent and then back at the baby. 'Was this something that only affected women?' He thought. He then held the baby as a nursing mother would and waited before placing the child back in the cot.

Despite her protests, Crooke had Elizabeth admitted to a private room and they stayed overnight. By morning, the agent was back to normal and well rested. Crooke stared out of the window at the peaks that surrounded them.

"Do you know that Hemingway is buried here?"

Elizabeth was seated on the edge of the bed and eating her breakfast and paused, "I didn't know; he shot himself didn't he?"

"Yeah, a sad ending to a brilliant career, but he loved walking in these mountains, and I can't say that I blame him," Crooke turned back to her, "Want to talk about what happened?"

Elizabeth finished eating and stood up, "I suddenly wasn't here, and with the sensation of falling into a bottomless pit. Glowing lights were flying in all directions. I think that I'm more tired than I realised."

"That was exactly what all of these mothers experienced," Crooke paused before asking the next question, "Do you want to try it again?"

The agent took a deep breath, and then nodded, "I'm game if you are!"

They found the baby fast asleep, but as Elizabeth entered the room, she became pale and sweaty. It took all of her willpower to approach the cot, but could not force herself to touch the sleeping babe.

"This is ridiculous!" she snapped, "I've faced armed maniacs and been shot, but I've never experienced this!"

"Describe what you're feeling right now." Crooke sounded intense.

"I'm standing on the edge of a precipice," she started to shake, "I've done skydiving, and it's always been a battle of will power to jump out, but this is far worse!"

"Okay, we'll go back to your room," Crooke relented, "I've been talking to this Doctor Jones and he's baffled. Fortunately, he hasn't heard about the other mothers, but that won't last long. What puzzles me is that when I picked up the baby, nothing happened to me."

"Then it must be that I'm too tired or something. How do the fathers react?" Elizabeth produced a wipe and used it on her face.

"The same as me."

"What about the female staff here, were there any incidents?" Elizabeth started to regain her colour.

"No one has reported any, and the nurses deal with him all the time."

"I think this is certainly weird enough to fit into our investigation." They reached her room, and Crooke had to ask her one more question,

"Do you want to continue and meet the other families? I would understand if you said no."

"I don't think that will happen again," Elizabeth put on her jacket, "I'm rested and ready to go."

"The next place is Sturgis, South Dakota, and a native American," Crooke informed her.

"Yeah I remember it, the father works in Ellsworth, and has a good income compared to many other Sioux and Cheyenne." Elizabeth recalled the notes, "That is not far from where that police officer talked to the aliens! Strange coincidence!"

They flew into Sturgis Municipal and drove out to the hospital. Charlie Dancing Snake looked just like any other American; he dressed the same, in jeans, and his black hair was cut short. He intercepted them in the corridor.

"Can you fix up my Fawn?" he was obviously very upset, "I want to call in our medicine man, but the hospital won't allow it."

"We're just as puzzled and worried as you," Crooke comforted him, "and if it comes to it, we may have to use your medicine man."

Elizabeth stared at Crooke, amazed that a man of science could resort to witchcraft.

Fawn lay in the bed in an almost comatose state but responded to Crooke's questions. "I don't understand it," her eyes were tearful, "Charlie and I wanted this child so much, but when I go near him, a great terror grabs hold of me."

"We know, we have your reports here," Elizabeth held up the folder, "As far as we can tell, you and the baby are in good health, and we just want to put things right."

"My sister has two children, and this has never happened to her, or anyone else we know," there was an anger boiling deep within Fawn.

"Can you describe what happened, how you felt?" Crooke asked.

"A great spirit came and paralysed me, and took me to a dark place, a place that our ancestors tell us existed before time, and I fell through it, and through the lights of the other spirits. I was very scared!"

"And since then, when you go to the child, what happens?" Crooke continued.

"I stand on a tall bluff, and below me is the darkness," fear showed in Fawn's face, "I can't see it, but I know it's there!"

"How would you feel if I allowed your medicine man in here?" Crooke asked.

Charlie answered him, "He wouldn't come; he says this is a bad place, and we would have to go to him."

"Why does he think that this is a bad place?" Crooke was genuinely interested.

Charlie shrugged, "He just says that there are bad things here."

"How does he know that?" Elizabeth was not convinced by voodoo.

"He used to work here, long ago." Charlie answered.

"As an orderly or a cleaner?" she continued.

"No, he went to college and worked here as a doctor," Charlie surprised them, "He has a regular clinic, and when we have a toothache, he pulls the tooth, when we have a fever he gives us penicillin.

When we are sick of heart, he will call on our old spirits."

Crooke thought that over; a modern doctor who also practised magic, "I'd like to meet him, but for the moment I'm going to arrange the release of Fawn and the baby so that you can go to him."

"No! He will kill the child!" Fawn shot up in bed and clawed at Crookes' arm, "He will believe that the child is evil!"

Charlie took Fawn in his arms, "He won't do that, and I won't let him."

This was not what Crooke expected or wanted. It was obvious to him that there was something psychologically wrong, and much of witchcraft is psychological. If Fawn would be willing to use the old beliefs, it could remove the revulsion - maybe.

"Okay, don't panic," he calmed her down, "I'll release you both, but if you don't want the old medicine, you don't have to have it. Do you have anyone to look after the child?"

Charlie nodded, "Her sister will do that for us."

"Good, now I would like to see the baby," Crooke stood in the doorway and took one last look at the distraught mother.

Elizabeth whispered to the doctor as they walked down the corridor, "Why were you advocating the use of the medicine man?"

Crooke returned the whisper, "This appears to be mainly psychological, and if it works it would be a good thing, at least for the mother. There is also a possibility that it would furnish us with more information."

The baby was sleeping, so Crooke gently revealed the navel. It was exactly like the other baby's; almost invisible, otherwise it looked normal.

"How do you feel at this moment?" he asked Elizabeth.

"Strangely tense, and I have a strong feeling that I should leave here at a run!" Her face was white and sweaty again.

"I don't think that there's any need to see more of these children or their mothers," Crooke decided, "I've seen enough, and I think that the remainder will be exact copies."

"I feel very relieved to hear that!" Elizabeth turned and walked out of the door, and then said something very unfeminine, "I prefer to be looking at facts rather than children. The sooner we're back, the better!"

Chapter Thirty-Eight

Martin Redfern was a chauffeur, but he didn't have to be. He had served his country with some distinction, being awarded the Silver Star and two Purple Hearts while in the Marines. He ended up in Fort Bragg as an instructor, and as he realised that he would probably not see action again, he got married, and they quickly had twins.

On leaving the Marines, he obtained the position as a security driver; delivering dignitaries and sometimes packages to various locations. The emphasis was on being low-key, and that's why most of the time he didn't drive a stretched limousine; his usual mount was a standard sedan but armoured. It was smaller, lighter, faster and more manoeuvrable than the grand behemoth, but more importantly, it was unnoticeable amongst the other traffic.

When he had thought about leaving the Marines, he had doubts about his future. He didn't want to work in an office or a factory; the monotony would have driven him mad! As a capable and well-trained soldier, he was offered this position, and he didn't have to work every day. True, he sometimes was called upon to drive for a week or more with the same 'package', and at inconvenient times, such as holidays and night-times, but overall it was a simple and relaxing work.

He had just taken his family on a tour of the Civil War battlefields in the family Volvo, compensating for a recent long absence from home, and taking the opportunity to teach his young children the nation's history. On some nights they slept under canvas, so that in the misty morning he could better describe the mornings before battle. His children were only three years old!

Today he was on standby; a visiting diplomat wasn't sure where he would be going or when, so Martin had picked up the car from the garage, and was driving it to the diplomat's hotel where he would await instructions.

The summer rush of tourists to Washington D.C. was almost over, but there was still enough traffic to negotiate; Washington was always busy! A pale-blue van pulled alongside him, and he automatically registered the occupants; two young Hispanics listening to music. At a junction just a few hundred yards further on, the van turned right, but in doing so it veered towards him, and the van and limo met with a glancing blow.

It was an everyday accident, but the van took off, and Martin saw red! His car was outfitted with some sophisticated communications, and normally he would have just informed the office, who would have in turn, informed the police, who would have picked up the van in a short time.

Martin floored the accelerator and turned savagely after the fleeing van, which had also picked up speed. He reached under his jacket and pulled out the 9-millimetre H&K pistol, laying it by his side.

He then punched the radio button, "This is Tango Three in pursuit of a suspected vehicle. Request back-up!"

There was a pause, and a puzzled voice answered him, "Vehicle just calling, please repeat your call-sign."

Martin swore, both at the radio and at a sleepy driver blocking his way, "This is Tango Three requesting back-up. In pursuit of a suspect vehicle, a blue van fleeing from a check-point." He side-swiped the slow car causing it to spin round. He just had time to notice the startled face of an elderly man.

"We don't have a Tango Three!" the radio crackled, "Is that you, Martin?"

"Yeah it's me, what's the problem?"

There was a long pause, "Where are you, Martin?"

"Heading on the north road," he rammed another car out of the way, "Suspects may have weapons, and I request a back-up." He was becoming frustrated with control, and the van was pulling away and becoming lost in the traffic.

He had lost both mirrors as he barged through the traffic, cars braking and spinning in all directions to get out of his way. He pulled up behind the van and leant out of the window, the H&K in his hand. The second shot blew out the van's rear tire, and it started to lose control but came to a sudden stop with its front wheels on the sidewalk.

Martin leapt out of the car and pulled the driver's door of the van open with a violent movement. The two Hispanics held their hands above their heads, their faces contorted in fear at the sight of the pistol. Martin yanked the driver out and slammed him face down on the sidewalk, and ordered the passenger to climb out and assume a position next to the driver.

That was the scene when the police arrived; Martin standing over the two men with a foot on one neck while covering the other man with his pistol. The police car had responded to calls about a madman speeding through the streets, and were more than a bit pissed at the carnage that had been caused on the Washington streets!

Martin was surprised when the two police officers disarmed him and placed him under arrest. His objections, including a few violent blows, were treated roughly as the handcuffs were applied, but the two Hispanics were ordered to stay on the ground until the situation could be resolved. Then a second police car arrived, this time called out by control, and that was followed by a plain car with Martin's boss.

"What were you doing Martin? Who is Tango Three?" he demanded.

Martin blinked and slowly looked around at the devastation, "I'm Tango Three Sir, or I think I am."

"What do you think this is?"

"I thought it was some Taliban up to something and was I pursuit," Martin was frowning and looking uncertain, "What happened here?"

The supervisor, Julius Spratt had seen this sort of thing before; Post Traumatic Stress Syndrome, a delayed reaction to a previous traumatic experience. He persuaded the police to remove the handcuffs and escorted Martin into the back seat of his car, "Just sit there, and I'll sort this out."

Martin was taken to a hospital and put under observation. The blocked freeway took a lot longer to sort out, and the two 'Taliban' turned out to be plumbers who were not concentrating on their driving.

Martin insisted that the van had fled a road-block, and that this happened in Iraq, not Washington. He couldn't work out how a chase that started in one country ended up in another, and that the Humvee he was driving turned into an ordinary car. The doctors had a tough time with him, and diagnosed that he was excessively aggressive and had to keep him sedated.

Chapter Thirty-Nine

"I've been looking at some of this data, and I think you're on a wild goose chase," Sheriff Reynolds said. He was talking to Donovan and Fallon, who had come down from Portland, as they met in Donovan's office.

"Why do you think that?" Donovan asked.

"You're looking for connections between all of these cases, and I can't see any." The sheriff slapped some papers down, "I wouldn't think that there would be as they are spread over all the country, so there's no chance that they knew the same people, went to the same stores, or even had their cars serviced in the same garage."

Fallon gave a slight cough and nodded, "What you say is true, and I'm not looking for any direct links between them. It's their behaviour, what they do that may be a common factor. Whatever this is has been spread across the country, and there must be a common factor for this to happen."

The sheriff grunted and shook his head, "Another point is that few of these events have any similarity, and can't be caused by one single thing."

"That's not exactly true," Donovan pointed out, "They have all suffered some mental aberration, and that has led to a different activity. We are all wired differently, and the effects will differ because of that."

The sheriff snorted in disbelief, "Something that makes us nuts; I won't believe it until you can prove it!"

"And that's exactly what we are trying to do!" Fallon continued tapping out on his notebook.

Fallon had arrived with another stack of CDs with more of the latest information. It was thought to be safer then e-mailing them, "All of these are cases where people have done unusual things. It reminds me of the Invasion of the Body Snatchers, except these are still the same people they were the day before, and the day after."

"I haven't seen any giant pea pods lying around!" the sheriff smiled at the thought.

"These people resumed acting normally, so we can dismiss that!" Donovan also smiled.

The door opened, and Elizabeth and Crooke entered.

"Hi, how'd it go with the mothers and babies?" Donovan asked.

"Interesting!" Crooke cocked an eye in Elizabeth's direction.

"I had an episode!" Elizabeth flung her briefcase down, and everyone went silent and blank-faced. This was unexpected!

"She saw exactly what the mothers reported seeing," Crooke had a sardonic twist to his mouth, "The really interesting thing is that none of the males and none of the female staff have experienced anything."

"So what makes me so different?" Elizabeth snapped back and sat down heavily.

"That is the real question," Crooke continued, "This may be a blessing, as we now have a victim that is trained to observe, and we can interrogate you at a greater depth than we can the others."

"Bring in the rubber hoses!" Elizabeth looked totally downcast.

Donovan was sifting through the reports on his computer, "It won't come to that, you saw an empty void with shooting lights and suffered vertigo," he looked up for confirmation, "I thought that there was some mental connectivity between mother and child, but you're not a mother."

"No, I'm not, and if this is what happens to mothers, I'll stay as I am!" Elizabeth slumped in a chair.

"We saw only two cases, and on the second one she felt very uncomfortable being in the same rooms as the child," Crooke said, "She had no problems with the mothers."

"What about the children; were there any abnormalities?" Donovan asked.

"Just the belly button," Crooke answered thoughtfully, "It's almost invisible. I can't remember seeing anything so small. I've brought back samples for testing, and I'm afraid to say it, but you need a thorough check-up as well Elizabeth."

She looked at him in surprise and then nodded, "As I am now an event, I suppose that's what should happen," she stood up, "Come on then!"

"There's no rush, you can rest tonight, and we do it tomorrow," Crooke said.

"Damn it! Do it now and get it over with! I suppose that I should remove myself from the case." Her face was pulled grimly back.

"I don't think so," Fallon had been watching and listening carefully, "If you are a victim of this, it would be more beneficial that you stay on the case so that we can see if anything else happens. Personally, I don't think it will!"

"Oh! I should at least inform the office and see what they think," Elizabeth said.

"I wouldn't if I were you," Donovan rose to his feet, "They will play for safety and remove you, and I agree with Fallon. In a real crime, murder or robbery, where you have a connection and could alter the evidence, I can see the justification, but in this case, you could supply vital evidence, and you can't alter these findings."

Elizabeth nodded slowly, "You're probably right. How are the background questionnaires coming on?"

Donovan lifted up some papers, "Slowly, and I don't think they are supplying everything we asked for."

"Not surprising," Elizabeth picked up her briefcase, "Witnesses are infamous for being unreliable. They probably think that some things are unimportant, like cleaning your teeth every morning, so don't include it. Come on Doctor; let's get the torture over with!"

Chapter Forty

Gerry made up for the shambles he made of the previous game, assisted by Joel and the rest of the gang. Joel was always a formidable opponent due to his size and strength, but this time he went further. The other team, Borland High, flung themselves at him, but with up to five players hanging on to him, Joel charged on at undiminished speed and shedding his opponents left and right. He passed the ball to Gerry at just the right moment, who drop-kicked from an enormous distance. Three times he passed the ball to Gerry, who performed the same drop-kick. On the fourth time, he passed to Billy and caught Borland on the wrong foot, and this left Billy and Sean with a clear run to the line. Ding-Dong was jumping up and down in ecstasy, despite the fact that his team had discarded his tactics and assumed their own.

This change of direction divided the Borland team, although they concentrated most of their players on Joel, who in turn treated them as though they didn't exist. He reminded Ding-Dong of a tank that ploughed through everything in its path! Joel varied his passes to the other three, and then in a burst of speed, surprising for someone so massive, he kept the ball and ran for the line. As a finale, he passed the ball to Gerry who made the longest drop-kick of the game. Borland didn't score at all! The watching crowd applauded the victors as the left the field, but Borland hardly had the energy left to do the same. They had been run ragged!

In the changing room, Ding-Dong couldn't stop smiling; a change from his usual dour countenance, "Well done boys! If you keep this up, we'll win the championship!" The team hardly heard him as they were more noisy and boisterous than ever as they entered the showers.

"Where did you learn to kick like that?" Billy asked Gerry.

Gerry shrugged, "It just looked like an easy shot, so I took it!"

Sean barged in with soapy water streaming down his face, "Easy my ass! I've never seen kicks taken from so far back; that was awesome!"

Billy shook his head, "Joel was awesome! He pulled most of the Borland players to him and made it easier for the rest of us. Have you ever seen a juggernaut like that?"

Joel heard him and turned round while under the shower, "I felt invincible, but those players weren't up to scratch; real fly-weights."

"Yeah, and you swatted them for sure!" Billy slapped him on a heavily bruised shoulder.

Marcus had been persuaded to film the game on a camcorder. Stills from this would be used in the school's magazine and the local paper. Marcus was surprisingly good with the camera.

The following day, Donovan watched the film in his office. It was quiet with Fallon plodding with the data in the corner, and the reporter took the advantage to catch up on his editorial work. Marcus had sent the film directly to Donovan's computer, and it was just one of several messages, so it was nearly lunch when he opened the file and studied the film.

"My God, you should see this!" he exclaimed.

Fallon looked up, "Something interesting?"

"It's the football game yesterday."

"I prefer baseball myself." Fallon sounded disappointed.

"Yeah, but it's our gang of lads in action," Donovan started the recording again, "If this were an army, they would flatten every enemy!"

Because it was related to some of the case subjects, Fallon got up and came to stand behind the reporter and look at the screen. Donovan pointed out Joel's charges, and the opponents bouncing off his massive frame.

"Look at that pass; Gerry leapt far higher than the others, and in the next one, Billy's arms seem to have grown an extension." Donovan felt like cheering, but he felt a nagging feeling in the back of his mind, "The other team were completely disorganised; they never expected our guys to be able to reach the passes, or that Joel would be so unstoppable."

"Is this exceptional play?" Fallon asked.

"Yeah, it is, and I wonder why." Donovan studied the film with a little crease between his eyebrows, "Joel was always unstoppable, but this is exceptional!"

"Do you think that it has something to do with the events?" Fallon could sense the reporter's consternation.

"I've started thinking that everything is an event!" Donovan ran a hand through his hair, "All of the events we have gathered up are different, except that they're all weird and unexplainable. This morning I wondered why my egg wasn't sunny side up! I think it's getting to me!"

Fallon patted his shoulder, "Don't worry my friend, in a few days we'll have an answer."

Donovan didn't look convinced, "I don't see how you can make sense of any of this."

"It is a difficult problem that uses several mathematical tools," Fallon returned to his desk, "There are many such tools that are often based on averages. It is a far too complicated procedure to explain now, but they will provide an area to investigate or several such areas."

"That's the point that I don't get," Donovan pulled a face, "We already have many conflicting events, and I can't see how you can isolate one factor."

"Ah, I see what you mean. We will not be able to tell you the name and address of the criminal, but we will be able to tell you the town he lives in if this were a criminal case. It reduces the workload from the impossible to the possible."

"It still leaves a lot of work for the FBI!"

"Or maybe it will be able to be precise, and we will not know that until we have finished." Fallon smiled, "Data is continuing to flow in, and it may not stop, so Demetrius will use that we have, which is considerable, and start using those tools very soon."

"I'm having a lot of difficulty with these questionnaires," Donovan flipped a pile of sheets,

"They are so vague with their answers that they are almost useless."

"When I have found a certain factor, you may be able to go back to them and ask a specific question, and then all will be much clearer."

Donovan looked at the top of the head as it bent to resume work, "I wish that I had your confidence!

Chapter Forty-One

"I thought we'd be seeing you fairly soon," Marcus spotted Donovan as he entered the Grill. The gang were still celebrating their victory, and they had been joined by Megan and Suzy.

"I thought that I'd find you here," replied Donovan as he sat next to the girls, "That was one amazing film!"

"Yeah, his middle name is Spielberg," Gerry vigorously ruffled Marcus's hair.

"Now you want to hear from the victorious heroes," Megan guessed.

"I'd be betraying my calling if I didn't ask a few questions. Joel, I can understand to some degree, he's like tackling a brick wall, but how on earth did you receive those passes?" Donovan caught the waitress's eye and ordered a coffee.

Gerry and Billy looked at one another and shrugged. The question hadn't occurred to them before now. Billy shrugged again, "I just went for it, and Joel's passes were dead-on. Does that answer it?" He aimed the answer both at Gerry for confirmation and Donovan.

"You should look at that film and ask that question again," Donovan sipped his coffee, "Some of the best pros in the business couldn't have reached those passes."

"Hell man! We're heading for the major leagues!" Joel's broad face split into a grin, and he performed a high five with Billy.

"If you can repeat it," Megan brought them down to earth.

Joel's grin disappeared and was replaced with a frown, "We did it once, so we can do it again."

"I spoke to coach, and he said that you didn't follow his game plan at all," Donovan watched carefully for their reaction, but they were just puzzled as to why he was asking the questions.

"As the game started, his plan didn't seem to be right, so we played it as we saw it." Billy defended the team.

"But you knew what the others were doing without any preconceived plan, and without signals; I watched that film carefully several times, and when the ball was passed, one of you appeared out of nowhere to receive it. Several passes were without the player being able to see where he was passing."

"You're saying it was a fluke!" Joel sounded indignant.

Donovan shook his head, "Do it again, and I'll form an opinion. Billy, how did you know that the ball was going to be where it went? On one occasion you started to run before Joel had even started to indicate he was throwing."

Billy looked blankly at the reporter and then at the others, "I can't answer that Mister Donovan."

"Perhaps it was ESP," Marcus volunteered.

Joel snorted, "And my granny's a Martian!"

"I'm not so sure that's bunkum." Megan placed a thoughtful finger on her chin, "Not that your granny's a Martian," she smiled at that, "but you boys have known each other since before school, and it's only natural that you could anticipate the other's moves."

"Something like that was on my mind," Donovan submitted that rather than what was really on his mind.

"You mean we can read each other's minds!" Gerry leant over to Megan, "Can you read what's on my mind?"

Megan's lips pressed into a tight line, "If you could read what's on my mind, you wouldn't sit so near!"

Donovan laughed with everyone else at Gerry's disappointed expression, "I'm not suggesting ESP, but that at certain times you appear to instinctively know what to do."

"I've read that when a couple have been married for a long time, they don't have to tell each other very much, they just know," Marcus said.

"That's it! You've known each other for about ninety-percent of your lives," Donovan felt relieved that the conversation went in the direction it did.

"Well honey-bunch, it's your turn with the dishes," Billy said to Gerry.

"Yeah, as usual, I'm chained to the kitchen!" Gerry replied.

Donovan left them to the usual banter and stepped out on to the sidewalk. What he didn't tell them was that some of the players were comparatively new to the team, and yet still managed to perform as well as the others. He had also been aware that both Megan and Marcus had watched him carefully. They also had thoughts they were not expressing!

Chapter Forty-Two

Jed Bates flexed his two hundred and fifty-pound body and downed the beer in a few seconds; then he ordered another. The bartender passed him the glass reluctantly and went to the other end of the bar where most of the other customers were avoiding any eye contact with Jed.

Logging can be a dangerous occupation, and Jed had two missing fingers and a scarred leg to prove it. Perhaps it was the pain that caused him to drink and pick fights, but everyone couldn't be bothered to make excuses for him, especially when he had a drink or four. He was heading for another bender, and the other customers drank up and headed for the door. Jed gave them a twisted smile as they passed him; he wasn't bothered what they thought.

The bartender eventually decided that Jed had enough, and in any case, he had driven off all of the other customers, and that meant that it was time to close. He reached under the bar and took a firm grip of the baseball bat that was kept there for just this reason.

"Okay Jed, it's a dead night, and I'm about to close up!"

Jed looked at him, "Give me one more beer and a chaser, and I'm gone." He knew why the bartender's hand was under the bar, and if it came to it, he would chew it into matchsticks.

He got his beer and chaser and stood up, "Take it easy, I'm off home to the little lady, and you can go to yours."

His four-by-four was as battered as he and its springs groaned as his bulk settled on the seat. On the way home he passed a patrol car, but it didn't cause him any problems; the officer knew what would happen if he pulled Jed over for drink driving.

When he pulled up at his house, he placed both hands over his face and rocked backwards and forwards. Then he looked up with an expression of bewilderment on his face; his pupils large and black. Shaking his head, he punched the steering wheel and flung the door open, and then slammed it shut so violently that it rocked on its worn out springs, and then he walked into a tree! Rising to his feet he staggered to the front door wondering from where the tree had come. It had been there for nearly a hundred years!

He stumbled his way to the kitchen and saw on the table a cold meal congealing in the fat on a plate. Red rage filled his face, and he whirled to see his slightly built wife Sara standing in the kitchen door with her arms folded and a sardonic expression on her face.

"You know that dinner was cooked hours ago, so you can eat what's left!" she spat out.

Jed's temper boiled over, and he lunged at her, only to find that she had moved quickly to one side and hit him with an axe handle – his axe handle! He collapsed on his hands and knees, partly from the blow and partly from having too many beers. He stood up clutching his back and turned round to see her standing in the hall with the axe handle pointing towards him.

Jed had been in too many brawls at work and in the bar to be intimidated, especially by a skinny wife! He lunged again, and this time she dropped the axe handle and grabbed his arm; the next thing he knew he was flying through the air and smashing through the front door. He cleared the stoop and hit the ground in a shower of wood splinters. He tried to stand up and realised that a shard of wood was sticking out of his thigh.

He roared and bellowed with rage, yanked out the wood, and holding the bloody shard like a dagger; he ran at his wife. She blocked his blow and deftly removed the makeshift dagger from his fingers, and then rammed it into his neck. Almost paralysed, he sank to the ground clutching his neck in surprise; where and when had she learned to disarm and strike back at a larger opponent? She had suffered at his hands for years without any sign of being capable of such actions.

The commotion had disturbed the neighbours who came out to see what was going on, and they were expecting to see Sara lying on the ground. They were so surprised they were struck dumb, but someone had the sense to ring the police, and the formerly reluctant officer who saw Jed pass earlier arrived on the scene.

Jed needed some urgent medical attention, and the ambulance quickly arrived, which was a good thing for him as no one else had come forward to assist. After all of the years of his abuse, they were not feeling obliged to offer him any form of help. Sara had struck deep in his neck severing several major nerves and arteries, and Jed was having trouble breathing and moving.

The officer had to take Sara to the station, but he didn't handcuff her. In his opinion and everyone else's, Jed had got what he had finally deserved after many years. Sara was questioned and released, backed up by the witness's statements of years of abuse. No one seemed interested in asking how she could have overcome her husband; there was nearly a two hundred pound difference between them!

Chapter Forty-Three

In all his years as a teacher, Hugh Pritchard had never been in this situation before! During his training and after, it had been explained to him that all he could ever expect is to teach the mediocre and nothing more. One of his associates had called the children 'cannon fodder' to be destined for nothing more than to feed the great machine called civilisation. Another more recently had alluded to teaching as 'mock pearls before real swine!'

Pritchard had never fully agreed with either of them. It was true that the majority would only fill the vacancies in industry, working on some dreary assembly line, but from time to time he had the satisfaction of introducing new ideas into young, receptive minds, and saw them flourish and develop into areas of medicine and law. Never had he expected to be dealing with the higher echelons of academia!

He had requested Marcus to come to his study, "Sit down Marcus, you're not in trouble. Make yourself comfortable."

The principal read the letter before him again, not quite believing what it said. He looked up at the young man before him who returned the look with a steady gaze. Marcus had a thin, almost skeletal body with a large head that was emphasised by his skinny body. A long face topped by an unruly mop of black hair and intelligent dark brown eyes framed by large spectacles. He looked the image of an immature professor!

Pritchard turned the letter round for Marcus to read, "I don't know how to say this, so you'd better read it for yourself."

Marcus read it carefully, his expression not changing as he did so. He looked up and gave an uncertain smile, "Princeton wants to evaluate me!"

Pritchard nodded, "Mr Gordon sent your records, including that work you did in class, to some people he knew, who then sent it to Princeton. Needless to say, they are impressed and frankly, so am I. I'm not a mathematician, and it's all above my level, but this could be the start of a brilliant career for you."

"Yes Sir, but I don't feel any different," Marcus had a sweaty sheen on his forehead.

"I wouldn't expect you to feel different, but this evaluation will open new avenues for you. What I would like you to do is go home and talk it over with your parents; I'll give you a copy of the letter because I'm sure they won't believe it either. What I want to stress is that we cannot teach you at that level here, and you need special attention to reach your full potential."

"I don't know if my parents can afford this," Marcus said quietly.

"I don't think that will be a problem," Pritchard smiled, "There will provision made, a scholarship or some such thing; impress your parents on that fact, and they should not worry. Well done and I'm very proud of you!"

Marcus left in a daze, and instead of going home as suggested, he sought out Gordy.

"I see that you've had the news," Gordy was all smiles, "what do you think?"

"At the moment I can't think!" Marcus wiped his forehead, "I feel there has been a mistake, and it's someone else they are talking about."

"Oh, it's you all right! What I would like to know is where you got that stuff from; I didn't teach it to you? You must have been reading at home."

"I've read bits here and there, but it just seemed to be logical at the time," Marcus shuffled his feet, "Have you any idea where this could go?"

"As far as you can take it!" Gordy slapped the boy on the shoulder, "I wish that it could have happened to me!"

His parents were working, so Marcus went for a long walk, reading the letter several times. He had often wondered what it would be like to be in a top university or any university, but now that it was here he was having doubts about his ability. Eventually, his feet took him to The Barbed Wire Grill, and he was drinking a soda when the gang came in.

"Where'd you go to? Have you been expelled?" they asked.

Marcus gave them a wry smile, "Kind of, at least I might be leaving the school."

"A punishment for showing up Gordy!" Gerry guessed.

"No, actually it's a reward!" Marcus giggled.

"Gee, I wish I could get that sort of reward!" Gerry slumped on a seat, "No more school, what a dream!"

"I said that I might be leaving this school, not school completely," Marcus felt brave enough to thump Gerry.

"Ignore these idiots and talk to me," Megan took his arm and snuggled in.

"Gordy sent that stuff I did on the board and my records to Princeton, and they want to evaluate me." He took a long draw on the soda.

Megan sat up with her eyes wide open, "THE Princeton, the place where Einstein worked?"

"Yup!" Marcus started to laugh softly, "I don't know what or how they evaluate, but they want to see me!"

He produced the letter and handed it to Megan, "This is amazing Marcus!" she said, "What do your folks say?"

"I haven't told them yet," he took back the letter, "I've been walking around and thinking; this is a big step."

"It's gynormous sport," Gerry got on his hands and knees and bowed to Marcus. Billy put his foot on his neck to keep him down.

"You are going?" Billy asked, "You'd be an idiot not to!"

"What if it was a fluke?" Marcus screwed his face up.

"Listen to someone bigger than you," Joel rumbled, "If you don't go, you'll curse yourself forever!"

"That was the conclusion I came to, but it scares the heebie-jeebies out of me!" Marcus licked his lips nervously.

"Did you speak to Gordy?" Megan asked, and Marcus nodded.

"There's that foreign guy over in Donovan's office doing something on the murder," Billy informed him, "He's a science geek like you, and I believe he's at least at the Princeton level. You could talk to him; he'll be impartial."

Marcus stared at Billy in surprise, "How on earth do you know what he's doing?"

"I have ways!" Billy touched his nose, "We met him in the Grill with Donovan, remember?"

"You were looking for that beautiful FBI agent!" Gerry got up from the floor and accused Billy indignantly.

"It's a good idea," Megan said, "The office is just over the road, and we can't help you and nor can your folks."

"Go for it sport!" Gerry rubbed his friend's hair, "Do you want us to come with you?"

Marcus shook his head, "Nah, this is something I have to do by myself."

"I'll come with you to give you moral support," Megan stood, "All these guys want is to see that FBI agent's legs!"

Donovan looked up in surprise as Megan and Marcus entered the outer office, "What can I do for you?"

Marcus didn't know where to start, so Megan spoke up, "Marcus has had an invitation to go to Princeton. Where's that letter?" She took the letter from Marcus's pocket and handed it to the reporter.

Donovan read the letter and then looked up, "This is great! How can I help?"

Marcus mumbled, "I'm not sure of what to do, and I heard that you've got a science guy working in here and I thought – the gang thought that he would give an impartial opinion."

"How on earth did you find out about him? Never mind, he's working in the back office, and I'm sure that he'll talk to you. You met him briefly in the Grill, his name is Demetrius, and he's a high-level mathematician, so he's a good choice," Donovan handed the letter back and stood up, "Follow me."

Demetrius read the letter and looked at Marcus quizzically, "You want to know what I think?"

Marcus nodded, "I've spoken to the school, but it's kudos for them, and therefore their opinion is biased. My friends are no better off than me, and I need some idea of what it will mean."

Demetrius nodded and sat back in his chair, "It's probably the biggest decision that you will ever make. May I ask you a few questions?" Marcus nodded.

"What does your father do for a living?"

"He's the town clerk." Marcus looked surprised at the question.

"Good! A stable job, and I suppose he organises things and so on. What does your mother do?"

"She used to be a musician, but now she teaches pre-school." Marcus looked more confused.

"This is good and does your mother play anything at home?"

"Usually just at weekends or on occasions she tinkers on the piano." Marcus looked hopelessly at Megan for support.

"Do you have many books in the home?"

Megan answered, "Marcus has more books than the town library! Okay, that's an exaggeration, but his dad built a study for him in the garden, and it's full of books. He's the brainiest person that I know of, and I'd put him against anyone in the state!"

Demetrius chuckled, "You have a champion! All of this is good, but you'll still find university life different than anything that you have experienced so far. Many of the students and staff come from academic families and have had private schools, tutors and that sort of thing. Classrooms can be just discussion groups where everyone contributes to an argument and debate; you'll have to defend vigorously any statement that you make, and there will be rivalries and jealousies that you will have to contend with. I don't suppose that you have had much in the way of argument."

"The only argument he gets is smart-ass comments from the gang," Megan agreed.

"That's what I am alluding to, and it goes on all of the time," the little Greek pointed a finger, "During a coffee break they will be talking about anything, and if you haven't had the background, you cannot participate. What are you reading at present?"

"I have several books that I'm currently reading, one is by Kant." Marcus was becoming fascinated in the conversation.

"Excellent, many of the arguments you will hear are about philosophy, the philosophy of mathematics, of science and any other subject. If you have read something on these, then you will not feel completely out of place. You have an enquiring mind, you seek knowledge and answers, and you'll fit in well at Princeton."

"Have you been there?" Marcus asked.

"I was lecturing there just a few months ago, "Demetrius answered, "I have a chair, a position in Thessaloniki, in Greece, but I have taken a sabbatical, a working holiday in the USA. Before that, I was doing some work for NASA, and now I'm working for the FBI. Once you have reached a certain level, the world is your oyster!"

Megan's mouth fell open, "NASA! Hey, guy, you could become an astronaut!"

Chapter Forty-Four

With a lot of hard work and some brilliant surgery, Crooke managed to save Jed's life, although for the time being the bully was comatose, and suspected to be at least partially paralysed. The blow that Sara had delivered to his neck had done a lot of damage to major nerves, and almost severing the spinal cord.

Crooke had removed the splinter of wood, and given it to the sheriff after giving it an examination. He was surprised that someone so slight as Sara could have driven the weapon so deep into Jed's thick neck, but it was just about the right size as a combat knife, and even resembled one in shape, and above all, it was extremely sharp. If Sara or anyone else had pulled the wood out, Jed would have bled to death in a few moments.

When he was first called out and saw what had happened, Crooke wondered if this was another event, but most of the damage appeared to have been caused by Jed, and the final blow was one of desperation by Sara after years of abuse.

Jed came round three days afterwards; the vague grunting noises alerting the attendant nurse. Jed was paralysed with only partial uncoordinated movement in his arms and legs, but his vital organs had regained some control, and he could be taken off the ventilator. When Crooke examined his eyes, all he could see was shouldering anger, and he shuddered; he had never encountered a real monster before!

Jed's vocalisation recovered, and he used his voice to hurl insults at the nurses and doctors, and as the swelling in his neck subsided, he recovered more use of his hands and legs. This simply made him impossible to deal with, and when he tried to remove the head and neck restraints, Crooke had no alternative than to tie down his limbs. It took Crooke, three large male nurses, and the sheriff who was just passing to hold him down while the straps were attached.

From that moment on, Jed spent his days and nights staring up at the ceiling while cursing everyone and everything in a constant stream of profanity. He followed the faint patterns in the ceiling tiles until he knew every shape that they made.

Now that Jed was immobile, Crooke could examine his wound which seemed to be healing well. He still had to be careful as Jed made an effort to bite the doctor's fingers, and for a proper examination a scan would be necessary, but while Jed was so aggressive, they could not let him free of his bonds.

On one night there was an electrical storm; the lights flickered, and for a few moments went out completely. A peal of thunder made the building shake, and Jed stopped cursing as he sensed a power greater than his.

In the indirect and faint light of the night lamps, he could make out that one of the ceiling patterns had developed into a crack directly over his bed. He concentrated on it, and saw that at each rumble of thunder it opened a little more. He screamed, but no one took any notice as he was always screaming. Sweat broke out over his whole body as he watched the crack widen.

A puff of smoke squirted out of the hole and drifted towards the door, then another. Jed screamed as loud as he could, but still no one came to see his problem; he was about to be crushed and burned, and he felt the terror of being helpless, as helpless as his many victims! He pulled at his restraints, trying to free himself and run from the room.

A tendril of smoke wound slowly out of the crack and descended to touch his face. He noticed that the core of the tendril was darker and denser. He had smelt and tasted smoke in forest fires and had his eyes burning from the fumes, but he had never experienced its touch before! It pushed and probed, entered his gaping mouth, eyes and ears. It plucked at his hair and then moved down his body. Other tendrils emerged from the crack and circled the room, curling round furniture and equipment. One wound itself round his bed and he could feel it tighten like a python before it lost interest and moved on the bed.

The tendrils of smoke kept coming, and now they were coloured, at first in pastel shades, but as they descended and moved about the room the colours deepened. Jed had stopped screaming and now just moaned in terror.

None of the staff wanted to deal with an unpleasant patient like Jed, so they restricted their care to looking through the window and saw that he was still mouthing something and writhing. They assumed that he was still the same and carried on with their other duties. Crooke came in and checked on the wound, and couldn't understand what Jed was saying. All that Jed saw was the coloured bands of smoke swirling around the doctor.

In the morning, Jed started to hear the sounds; vague echoes from a long distance like whispers in a tunnel. Then the sounds became voices that called his name. Some of them sounded like his mother and father, and another like his long departed sister. After a few more hours the voices became more distinct and accused him of horrors, some he had done, and others he had only thought of.

Jed was in a perpetual sweat and his breath was coming in short bursts. He writhed all the harder, but the smoke continued to swirl around the room, and the voices continued, sometimes rising to shrill screams.

He finally lost it when the smoke began to take the forms of people; faces distorted as though they were reflected in funny mirrors, twisting into horrible caricatures of human figures and hellish monsters. Only then did he lay still and stop mumbling, just his eyes darted around as they followed the frightening shapes.

Crooke came in on his morning rounds and saw immediately that something had changed. Physically, Jed was in good shape; the vital signs were excellent apart from a slight fever. The wound was healing well, and the swelling had subsided, and the doctor and nurse had no trouble in taking readings. However, Jed failed to respond to questions or even look at Crooke, his eyes on a restless search all-round the room.

Crooke undid the patient's restraints and Jed just laid there, no swearing or trying to fight. Frowning, Crooke ran through the checks again and confirmed that Jed was improving physically, and had regained more of his motor functions. The day before he would have tried to leap off the bed and attack the nearest person.

Jed's future had been a recovery followed by a long spell in prison for beating Sara, but now he would be transferred to a psychiatric unit for perhaps an even longer period. Crooke was sure that Jed Bates had lost his marbles!

Donovan hovered around to get something he could use in an article, and he had questions about the incident; was it one of the cases?

Crooke thought about it. "Very possible! You should see his wife Sara, and then the damage to the house. I can believe that Jed caused the damage, he's all muscle and bone, but not a skinny little girl like her!"

"I have seen the damage, and I talked to the neighbours and the cop that came there. It would appear that the skinny wife threw the hulking brute through the air for some distance." Donovan looked at the doctor with a strange expression on his face, "If that isn't something very strange and remarkable, then I'm a Dutchman!"

Chapter Forty-Five

The weather had changed, and the first of winter's icy winds cut through Elizabeth's clothing. As a southern girl, she didn't appreciate the northern climate, although she had worked there for years. She had decided to walk from the motel to Donovan's office and quickly realised that it was not a good idea.

She sighed with relief when she entered and closed the door. Donovan looked up and smiled as he realised what had happened.

"You should get some clothing from the local store; you'll find it much better."

"Better still, I could get a transfer back to Georgia!" she dropped into a chair and rubbed her hands.

"I'll get you a coffee," Donovan fetched a mug, "We can get some killer winds, and you should be careful, being that you're a southern flower."

Elizabeth smiled as she accepted the mug, "Thanks for the coffee, and the compliment."

"Demetrius thinks that he has enough data to get some results," Donovan nodded towards the back office where the Greek could be seen bent over the keyboard.

"I hope so," Elizabeth put her coffee down firmly, "I've had instructions to wind this up as soon as possible. My chiefs think that this is a wild goose chase, and I'm almost inclined to agree with them."

"You will agree that there are some very peculiar things happening?" the reporter dropped into his chair, "When I look at these reports, I must say that I can't see a connection, but I then think 'Why are these happening in just a belt across the country'."

"That's my argument, and since they haven't an answer, they've allowed this to wind down rather than abruptly stop."

"That would create suspicion and comments," Donovan jabbed a pencil at a stack of papers, "There are already conspiracy theories and stories about aliens. Fortunately, they don't connect anything."

"Did you hear about that drunken brute that his wife put into the hospital?" Elizabeth held the mug with both hands to get some warmth.

"Yeah, Jed Bates keeps getting a mention in the paper from time to time. I understand that he's off to a long stay in a funny farm; serves him right!" Donovan lowered his voice, "There are a lot of stories about him and his old man going back many years."

"What sort of stories?"

"Nothing was proved, but the general consensus of opinion is that they were both responsible for a series of disappearances, mostly campers and hikers, and there are serious questions about his long lost sister. At that time the family lived way out of town in a shack. Bates senior arrived here from God knows where with his wife, and Jed was born shortly after. From day one, Papa Bates had the reputation of starting bar fights and being generally unsociable, and Jed is a carbon copy."

"Do you think that they fit into one of the events?"

Donovan shook his head, "It started long before these events, but there is one question on my mind."

"And that is?" Elizabeth raised her eyebrows.

"His wife Sara is an itsy-bitsy slip of a girl, and yet she managed to overpower a hulk like Jed, threw him out of the house through a closed door!"

"But she used a sharp weapon," Elizabeth pointed out, "That would have equalised things a lot."

"But Jed was covered with a lot of bruises, head, back and arms. From what I understand, the sharp weapon was used after she threw him!"

"Was anyone else there?"

Donovan shook his head again, "That would be a reasonable assumption, but there isn't anyone in the area that would stand up to Jed. No sign of anyone else there. I think that Sara could be an event!"

Elizabeth sat back and sipped her coffee as she thought through what Donovan had said. Super-human strength would be unusual, and just as weird as all the other events.

"Whatever, we have to come to some conclusion within a few weeks," she looked over to the top of Demetrius' head, "How's he doing?"

"Let's ask him and tell him that time's run out."

Demetrius didn't seem at all put out by the news, "I should have some results in a day or two. You must understand that I can only show strong possibilities and that there may be several to choose from."

"That's better than none at all!" Elizabeth muttered.

"I promise that you will have a clearer picture when I have finished, but it may still be a little confusing." The Greek turned back to the computer.

"Well, I'd better tell the good news to the sheriff and Crooke," Elizabeth said.

"Take my car," Donovan offered, "You'll freeze to death otherwise."

The sheriff was out, so Elizabeth continued to the hospital and told Crooke about closing the program down.

"I can't make any sense of it," the doctor exclaimed, "Nearly all of the events have no similarities. If we think of one of our earlier guesses that something was dropped from an aircraft, all of the victims would have shown the same symptoms, sneezing, coughing, maybe a skin rash, but they would all be the same. None of these are like that!"

"Except the new children!" Elizabeth reminded him.

Crooke nodded, "Except the children, and that just adds to the puzzle."

"Demetrius will hopefully provide an explanation," Elizabeth changed tack, "Did you deal with that bully?"

"Jed Bates? Yeah, I did, and I don't have any sympathy for the monster! Several times his wife was in here with some horrific damage, broken ribs and arms and once her jaw was dislocated."

"How did she overpower him?" Elizabeth asked.

"I'm not sure that she did," Crooke surprised the agent with his reply, "He flew through the door, and I can't see how she could have done that!"

"He could have charged, and she stepped aside," Elizabeth suggested.

"It was the top of the door that took the impact, and if he had charged it should have been the bottom and middle of the door, plus he was covered in bruises that didn't come from running into anything."

"Do you think that someone else was there?"

Crooke shrugged, "It's not my problem now, nor Sara's. Whoever it was has done humanity a service!"

Chapter Forty-Six

"I have produced some results." Demetrius smiled at the group gathered in Donovan's office, "I need to feed it to you in pieces, and this is the first," he turned the laptop round so that everyone could see and what they saw was the screen divided diagonally, the lower part a solid black.

"This is all of the data that is complete so far, including the fully answered questionnaires, placed on a bar chart. There's still a mass of data to enter, so it's incomplete," Demetrius pointed to the screen, "The reason it looks solid black is because of the amount of data and how I arranged it. On the left we have details such as where they lived, income, etc., in the middle are the gender of the subjects; that works out at about equal and then we come to the right-hand column," he enlarged the view, and the bars became separated, with the last topped by a number, "This is what they all did, one hundred percent!"

"And what was that?" the sheriff asked.

"Camping! All of the subjects spent some time in the wilds since the start of summer." Demetrius looked triumphant.

"That's not much good!" the sheriff snorted, "Unless they all camped in the same place."

"Unfortunately, they went all over, but only within the area of the belt, which I shall call the Zone. There's something in the forests apart from bears," the Greek wasn't put out by the sheriff's comments.

"It doesn't help us at all!" Elizabeth frowned.

"Worse than that," Crooke added, "There must have been thousands camping during that period; it's almost a national past-time!"

Donovan reached the obvious conclusion, "If that's the case, there are many more events that we know nothing about!"

Demetrius nodded vigorously, "The data has revealed the possible size of the problem, something that we were unaware of until now."

The group was struck dumb as the implications sank in.

"There's no way that my chiefs would accept that! We have to narrow it down a lot more." Elizabeth pointed to the screen, "What are these that are almost at the same level?"

"The next is IQ, where we could measure it, and it's only seventy-six percent of the population that is over one hundred," Demetrius looked slightly less than confident, "I must admit that some of this was guessed at judging from their employment."

"I don't get it!" Sheriff Reynolds placed his hands on his hips and glared at Demetrius, "Those newborn kids hadn't been camping, and the drug lord doesn't seem to fit into any of this."

"Ah, but their parents had been camping, and at just the right time and place." Demetrius smiled even broader, "What we are looking for is something that parents can pick up and transmit to the unborn, and as for the drug lord, he must have been intelligent because he was successful at his chosen profession."

"You're talking about a virus, but I don't know of any virus or a bacterium that produces these results," Crooke said.

"I agree!" the sheriff glowered at them with his hands on his hips, "We have a drug lord murderer, a junior Einstein, a crack football team, people having strange visions, and peculiar births. There's nothing in my book that can do all those!"

"But it does narrow the field by quite a lot," Elizabeth brightened up, "We need to look at something that can lead us to a more precise culprit."

"That I have an idea about," Demetrius closed the laptop, "Before I say anything I will have to confer with a few friends, so I'm going to be absent for a few days."

"I can say that we have started to make progress," Elizabeth smiled for the first time, "You go ahead, and I'll try to prolong the investigation."

Chapter Forty-Seven

The gang were passing a medicine ball to one another in the park. They made passing the heavy ball look easy, but Megan and Suzy knew better and stayed on a bench.

"There something odd going on," Billy grunted as he took the full force of the ball, "Has anyone heard anything more about that Mexican?"

"No, but the FBI are still here," Sean replied.

"She's fascinated by my personality!" Gerry passed the ball to Sean by swiping it with his forearms.

"In your dreams Romeo!" Billy laughed.

"Capulet!" Gerry sneered.

"Montague!" Billy replied.

"I didn't know that you'd read Shakespeare," Megan called out.

"Gerry had a comic book for Christmas," Sean said.

"No, I saw the movie," Gerry replied.

"Has anyone heard from Marcus?" Joel bounced the ball off his chest towards Billy.

"I've got his cell phone number," Megan called out.

"Give him a ring and see how he's doing," Gerry yelled back.

Marcus had left for Princeton the previous week, and since then there had been no word from him.

"Do you think they're picking him to pieces? Torturing him on some fiendish machine!" Gerry looked happy at the thought.

"You should look at other programs on the TV Bud, it's twisting your mind," Joel growled.

"Thanks! Last week you said I hadn't got a mind! It's an improvement" Gerry dropped the ball.

"What we said was that you had a single track mind," Billy did some squats as he could feel the tension building up in his back and thighs.

"There's more than one track?" Gerry looked suitably amazed.

"He's not answering," Megan called out, "I guess he's busy."

"Being strung out on a giant rack," Gerry licked his lips.

"That's what I mean," Joel growled again, "All you think about is giant racks!"

Billy collapsed laughing, and that signalled the end of the session, "You guys tear me up!"

They walked back to the girls and pulled out some soda cans from a chill bag.

"I'll ring later," Megan looked thoughtfully at her cell phone, "Unless he isn't allowed a phone."

"It's a university, not San Quentin!" Billy said, "He's tied up, try at dinner time."

"Getting back to Gerry's girlfriend," Sean took a swig from the can, "She's been here for a hell of a long time, and I don't believe it's because she's fascinated by any of us."

"She likes Donovan," Suzy said, "I see them a lot together, as I live opposite the motel."

"The fiend!" Gerry struck a pose, "I'll challenge him to a duel!"

"What with, powder puffs?" Joel reached up and pulled Gerry down.

It wasn't until much later when they had gathered in the Grill once more that contact was made with Marcus on the telephone.

"Gerry wants to know 'are they torturing you?'" Megan asked.

"Kinda, they're giving me a load of tests and some calculations I've never heard of before. It makes my head spin just trying to understand. They try to explain anything that I don't understand, and that's for most of the time."

"Something our genius doesn't understand! Wow!" Gerry looked genuinely surprised.

"I heard that!" Marcus said, "There are some really fantastic people here. I join into lectures and discussion groups, but sometimes I just don't understand a thing. It's as though there's something just out of reach, but I'm having a great time, and I hope it continues for a while. I miss you guys!"

"How's the food?" Sean asked.

"Great, but they have different themes, tonight it's Armenian."

"Have they given you sheep's eyes yet?" Gerry became gruesome again and smacked his lips.

"Not yet, but as they say in physics 'nothing's impossible!'" They all heard him chuckle.

"I understand that you don't know when you're coming back?" Billy asked.

"I'll be home for Thanksgiving, or my mom with raise hell! I'll see you morons then!" and Marcus signed off.

"Did he just call us morons?" Gerry said indignantly.

"We all call you a moron, moron!" Joel chuckled.

"That's okay then!" Gerry assumed a stupid expression.

"Can we get back to the lady with the long legs?" Megan asked.

"Oh yeah," Gerry's expression changed to one of rapture, "I can get back to her anytime!"

Megan pushed him over, "She has been here for nearly a year, and I can't see her superiors allowing that time because she's fascinated with Donovan, or even our young sex maniac here. Nor do I think she is specifically interested in the death of the drug lord or Old Hamish. So why is she here?"

Billy pulled on his ear, "This isn't exactly a place like the old Chicago with Capone calling the shots, in fact, there's very little happening most of the time. There aren't many strangers in town if any, and I haven't noticed cannabis factories or know of anyone doing anything illegal."

Megan took her time to answer, "The only other things we know about are Suzy's little stunt, Marcus becoming even brainier, Joel and Gerry's misplaced memory and their prodigious performance on the field."

There was a pause while they thought about that, even Gerry had gone quiet. Finally, Billy spoke up, "If we add to that the drug lord and Old Hamish, we have a collection of weird things. Why does she spend more time with Donovan than the sheriff? I don't think it's totally romantic, and the other person she spends a lot of time with is Doc Crooke."

"You forgot the little guy in Donovan's office, hammering away on a computer," Megan reminded them, "Where does all that lead us?"

Sean had been keeping quiet during all of this; he always was reticent about speaking out, but now he added his thoughts, "What if we stop thinking of them as people, but more as functions? Donovan collects and distributes information, a computer does the same and can work on that information," he paused, "Doc is a bit off centre, but he does gather information of a particular type, and the FBI monitors what is going on. I think that it's an information task as the sheriff also acts on information, although he doesn't actively collect it."

Joel's forehead creased, "What information?"

"You, Gerry, Suzy and Marcus," Megan looked up from her hands which had been fiddling, "We had an investigation into our medical status, a deep one that included our IQs, and our long legged agent appeared just before that happened."

"Those medical checks are nation-wide and not just here!" Gerry objected.

"That simply indicates that whatever it is, it's nation-wide," Billy answered.

"You forget the plane crash," Megan reminded them, "There were a lot of medical investigations over that! If there was a plane crash!"

"I think we're drifting into conspiracy theories," Billy warned them.

"How the hell can we find out something without a name over the whole USA?" Gerry had dropped his comic act for a while.

"Perhaps it's something that Donovan would have easy access to!" Megan suggested.

"Donovan collects stories," Billy looked thoughtful, "and they are about everything and anything, and he has access to all sorts of places. I still have no idea of what to look for!"

Megan looked triumphant, "That's easy! Suzy, Joel, Gerry and Marcus, you can throw in Old Hamish and the drug lord as well. We are looking for weird things!"

"Where are we going to find that?" Gerry looked uncharacteristically serious.

"The same place as Donovan, in the newspapers," Megan stood up, "We can look at back issues in the library, and we only have to go back to the spring or summer when everything started to happen."

Billy stood with her, "We can look in the whole state to begin with, and then move out to other states."

The librarian looked up as they entered the library, and then looked suspiciously at the gang when they asked to see back issues of newspapers over the whole state. She explained that they only kept hard copies for a month, and anything earlier would be on microfiche.

Joel looked down at her and tried to look intelligent, "That's okay Miss, just show us what to do," he rumbled.

Chapter Forty-Eight

Father Martin O'Brien of All Saints Church had looked after his parish for twenty years and enjoyed every moment. On the whole, they were good people, but he had problems getting them into the church. It was a matter of the only times he saw a full church was in 'hatchings, matchings and dispatchings', but that was fairly normal for almost every congregation of any persuasion.

He would greet people in the street, and when they were in need, he would offer his services, whether they were Catholic or not. Without exception, everyone respected the cleric as an honest and kindly person.

He had decided to enter the church at an early age, just fifteen. He was well aware that the religion had a horrendous history, and he didn't believe in the gospels, not entirely. Commonsense told him that many of the miracles were an impossibility, and history has shown that many had been passed down from more ancient societies while the Jews were captives. He did believe in the Christian code of being kind and generous, not so much with money, but with one's time and understanding.

He was therefore understandably shocked when one morning he found the Devil waiting in the vestry! It looked like the Devil, red all over and horned, its tail swishing back and forth as it sat cross-legged on the corner of a table. The face was dog-like with large canines protruding from the almost invisible upper lip, but the eyes were more feline; yellow and with slitted pupils. Even more revolting to the priest was the enormous penis that was semi-erectile.

"Hello Martin," the apparition hissed, "I've been waiting for you!"

Father O'Brien's blood ran cold. What could the Devil be wanting with him, a man of God who had done no one harm? He didn't believe in Hell or the Devil; they were features in the nature of mankind. He tried to reply, but his mouth had become dry.

"You never believed in Old Satan, Beelzebub, and Lucifer; well here I am!" The apparition gave a wheezing chuckle.

The priest sank to his knees as the strength went out of his legs, and automatically he brought his hands together with the rosary and started to pray.

"There's no need to kneel before me Martin; I'm not as demanding as that fraud you worship." A wisp of smoke trickled out of the elongated snout. "In a few minutes, Miss Bailey will enter to start cleaning the church; isn't she a beauty? Why don't you invite her in here, and we can both get to know her, biblically speaking?"

O'Brien continued praying, the sweat pouring down his face.

"Or perhaps on the altar, she can be your first sacrifice! I know that you want her and that you've had wishful thoughts about those heaving teats and generous thighs, and she has similar thoughts about you, how you would fondle her breasts. Take her now and realise your dreams!" The laugh that the Devil produced was dry and rattled in the throat, like the last breath of a dying man.

Father O'Brien heard the latch on the church door clatter, and the hinges creak as Miss Bailey entered. What the Devil had said was true; he had romantic thoughts about her, but what the Devil was saying was pure lust, the bestial taking of another person, no love or sharing. He rose from the floor and took a swipe at the scarlet demon – and found nothing! The Devil had vanished!

He tottered out of the vestry and towards the door, "There's no need for you today Violet. Come back tomorrow."

Violet Bailey looked surprised, and then noticed the priests face, "Why Father, you look ill; shall I fetch some help?"

"No, no, I'm alright, just a little indigestion," the priest clutched his stomach. It was true that his stomach was in turmoil. All of his beliefs of a lifetime had been shaken in a few moments!

"You sit down right there, and I'll go and get some medicine from the drugstore." She didn't believe that the Father had just indigestion; she'd never seen a face like that before.

"Don't fuss yourself, I'll be okay in a few moments," he gave her a shaky smile.

"Nonsense! You'll need something more than to sit down. I'll be back before you know it."

As she left, Father O'Brien looked nervously around the church, but there was no red figure or sibilant whisperings. He looked up at the roof just to see if the nightmare was hiding there. Then for the first time in his life, he went to the altar and prayed with full conviction!

It was noticed that he became distracted and not paying the usual attention during conversations over the next few days, and all the time looking nervously over his shoulder. During a sermon he would suddenly stop and stare at a woman who wore a red dress, or if someone spoke in a loud whisper.

His faith had been shaken, not in the church, but in himself. What had happened? The rational part of his mind said that devils didn't exist and nor do angels. Was that the reason, he didn't believe in the scriptures enough to be a priest? Are there really powers out there beyond his comprehension? Was his commitment being tested?

He took down his personal copy of the Bible and sat at his desk. He had also taken down a book on the science of creation, the Big Bang, and held that in his left hand. On the shelves, he also had the Bhagavad Gita, the Popol Vuh, the Koran, and the Talmud, and many more in his efforts to understand people and faith.

He sat for half an hour weighing the two books in his hands and thinking of their conflicting contents. In despair he groaned and rang the archbishop, explaining that he had some troubles and needed to talk to someone. He was invited to bring his troubles and assured that all would be resolved.

Father O'Brien found it difficult to explain what had happened when he arrived. The visitation of the Devil was easily said, even if it did raise the archbishop's eyebrows, but in talking about his deepest thoughts, and the struggle he was in became more and more difficult; he stammered and faltered all the way through, the archbishop waiting patiently until the end before speaking.

"My Dear Martin, you had these doubts from the first time we met, and I thought that I made it clear that it was possible to believe in God and science; one is fact, and the other is faith. I suspect that what you have experienced is a kind of epiphany, a realisation that your faith was weak, and that God is putting that right."

"I could understand that if I had seen a blinding light like Saint Paul, or hear a heavenly choir, but I saw the Devil himself!" Martin was starting to feel better just to get the matter off his chest and into the open, "I'm wondering if I am fit to serve the Lord."

"Just because you ask the question makes me believe that you are," the archbishop smiled kindly, "We all go through this at some time or other, and we are human and have those desires that we must control. I think that your faith is all the stronger for the experience, as you have followed the path of Christ and St. John the Baptist as they searched for the answers in the wilderness; you can consider that you have been in your own wilderness until now."

"But Satan was as real to me as you are now," Martin wrung his hands, "How can it be possible for this to happen? It's impossible for a creature to appear out of thin air!"

"I think that in physics there is a theory that matter can appear from nowhere, I believe they are called virtual particles," The archbishop paused as Martin looked up in amazement, and then continued, "I too read about science, so don't be astonished! This theory is well believed, and much of science is an act of faith until it is proved, and I can see no difference in faith in science or faith in God."

"This wasn't a particle, it was a creature!" cried out Martin, his eyes large and full of tears.

"I think that it was a manifestation from your mind, a result of inner turmoil that was being resolved," the archbishop took one of Martin's hands, "You should consider yourself blessed to have achieved this level of enlightenment. Now, when was it you last confessed your sins?"

The archbishop would have been less confident if he had been with Martin on the return journey. Just as Martin pulled on to the freeway, he looked in the rear-view mirror and saw yellow eyes staring back at him. He just managed to correct a violent swerve and then looked over his shoulder. The back seat was empty! He sighed and looked forward and on the dash was a miniature Devil.

"Do you feel better for your little chat? Do you now think that your faith is all the stronger?" Satan sniggered, "Do you still think of those swelling breasts and secret place between the thighs?"

"Satan, be gone with you!" Martin yelled.

The figure disappeared only to reappear full size in the passenger seat, "Anger is good, it's human. So are tits and thighs and buttocks and balls and dicks, very human."

Martin stamped hard on the brakes, and the unperturbed Devil slid forward through the windscreen and stopped in the middle of the hood. It turned and smiled at the priest, "Fine vehicles they have today, so much better than the old chariots when we pulled the Christian women apart in the arena, displaying all of their charms to the world."

Martin screamed and floored the accelerator. A few minutes later he drove directly at a tanker, and the ensuing inferno would have done Hell justice! Witnesses stated that Martin had sped past them, screaming and waving his fist at something ahead.

Not much of this came to the immediate attention of the FBI as confessions are confidential.

Chapter Forty-Nine

"Have you heard what happened to Father O'Brien?" Suzy ran into the gang on the street going into the library.

"No, we've been to practice all afternoon," Billy replied.

"He's been in a car accident! I hear that he hit a tanker and the whole thing blew up," Suzy's eyes filled. She was a devout Catholic and knew the priest well.

The surprise and horror showed on the gang's faces; Father O'Brien used to be a supporter of the team, and gave them a blessing before each game, even though most of them were not of his church.

Billy and Sean sat down heavily on the library steps, "How the hell did that happen?" Billy scowled.

"I don't know the details," Suzy held her hands out in a helpless gesture.

"I wonder if they know anything in here," Megan turned towards the library, "or we can go and ask Donovan or the sheriff."

"Donovan gets to know most things quickly," Billy leapt to his feet and headed towards Donovan's office. The others were startled into action and scurried after him.

Donovan looked up in surprise as the gang burst through the door led by Billy.

"Have you heard about Father O'Brien?" Billy burst out.

Donovan slowly put down the papers concerning the accident that he had been reading, and studied the gang's faces; obviously, they were upset. The younger girl, Suzy was the most affected.

"Yeah, I've just got the report in," He had no intention of filling in the details, especially in front of Suzy, "He was coming back from seeing his archbishop, and was in a collision with a truck; he died instantly, so they say."

"We heard that it was a tanker," Billy leant forward with his knuckles on the reporter's desk, "How did it happen?"

Donovan pulled a face, "It would appear that Father O'Brien was driving too fast on the wrong side of the road."

"I don't believe that!" Joel rumbled from the back of the group, "I've been with him in a car, and I can't think of a safer driver!"

"I've never known him to speed, even in an emergency," Suzy whispered, and the rest agreed with her.

"I've only got the reports to go on, and early statements are often changed on further investigation," Donovan tried to sound positive, but it didn't really come across, "If it's any consolation, I find it hard to believe as well."

"That's another weird thing that's happened this year!" Megan had an expression of anger mixed with confusion and something else. Donovan took another look at her. As a girl, she wasn't outstanding in a crowd of jocks, even though she was a good looking girl, but now that Marcus was not part of the group, she was beginning to show her intelligence, and it was a different type of intelligence to the rest, probably because she was female.

"He'll be missed, that's for sure," Donovan tried to avoid going in the direction that the gang's questions were going, "He was here before all of you were born, and before I came here. I'll write something very special for him."

"We can all write a tribute to him," Gerry surprised everyone with a sensible suggestion.

"That's a damn good idea!" Donovan silently thanked him for changing the conversation's direction, "Get them into me as soon as possible, and I'll include them." He stood up indicating that he had something to do and the discussion was over, but Megan had folded her arms over her bosom and was frowning at the floor. He suspected that she had seen that he was avoiding her unspoken questions.

Megan continued frowning as they returned to the library.

"What's up with you? You've a face like a thunder storm," Billy tried to put his arm around her shoulders, but she shrugged him off.

"He didn't want to answer our questions! Didn't you notice?" Megan spat the words out.

"I didn't see that. I thought that he was really concerned about Father O'Brien." Billy was puzzled at his friend's mood, and the others had gone quiet.

"He was obviously, but he didn't tell us everything," Megan looked directly into his face, "He didn't respond to my statement about weird things happening."

"How should he respond?" Billy looked confused.

"As he didn't, I can't say, but he should have agreed, disagreed or something in between."

Billy couldn't make up his mind if she had something, or was just being paranoid or just upset, so he said nothing.

Father O'Brien's funeral was a grand affair! The whole town turned out at All Saints Church, and the service was conducted by the Archbishop, who seemed more than a little disturbed. Eulogies were read by the mayor, the Baptist minister, the school principal and the chairman of the local business group. Father O'Brien had influenced so many people in all walks of life, and his passing would leave a large vacuum, and so many people had turned up that most of them had stood outside amongst the tombstones and trees listening to the service through loud-speakers.

Billy and the gang stood on the edge of the crowd, and from that position he was surprised to see Elizabeth and Fallon in the large crowd. Were they just being polite or was there some other reason? He saw Donovan and Crooke whispering to each other, and Billy wondered what they were saying. Was there something in what Megan said? He saw Megan and Suzy and edged over to them.

"Hell of a turnout!" he said to them.

Megan nodded and appeared to have recovered from her outburst, "Perhaps you should use another expletive! The Barbed Wire Grill is laying on a free buffet and drinks afterwards. Do you see who's in the crowd?"

"You mean the FBI, yeah I noticed them, and can you see Donovan and Crooke over there?" Billy nodded towards the whispering pair, "I wouldn't have given either of them a thought, but you could be right."

"I know I'm right!" Megan said still with a hint of anger, "They are not telling us the whole story, maybe none of it at all!"

Suzy sniffed into her handkerchief, and her eyes were red from constantly crying, "Why would they lie to us?"

"If we knew what it was, we would know why they're lying," Megan explained.

"I think they've finished all of the speeches," Billy pointed, "Shall we see if they'll give me a beer at the Grill?"

Chapter Fifty

Crooke, Donovan and the FBI didn't go to the Grill. Instead, they gathered in the sheriff's office. It was cramped with all of them present, and they occupied all the chairs and desks. Donovan remained standing.

"What's so important?" Elizabeth complained. She'd been looking forward to a few cocktails and meeting the inhabitants informally. People say a lot when emotion and alcohol are involved.

Donovan started to explain, "Crooke here has some sensitive information about Father O'Brien…"

"It's sensitive because it concerns the privacy of the confessional," Crooke interrupted and took over the narrative, "O'Brien went to the archbishop that day because he had some personal problems, and I had a lot of trouble getting anything out of the archbishop. In the end, I had to tell him part of what we are doing so that he realised how serious it could be. I finally clinched it by pointing out that doctors also were bound by a code of confidentiality, and finally I got most of the story."

"So what was troubling O'Brien?" Fallon asked.

"He met the Devil!" Crooke smiled at the look of surprise on everyone's faces, "Think of what that could mean to a man of faith before you pour cold water on the idea. After I had told him that this was a possible world-wide problem, the archbishop broke into a sweat because he connected what O'Brien had said, and thought that I was referring to the coming of the anti-Christ."

"Poor man!" Elizabeth murmured from where she sat in the sheriff's chair, and she looked as though she meant it.

"I'm not sure that the thought has completely left him, even after my explanation," Crooke agreed, "Did you notice how flustered he was during the service?"

"So what did the archbishop say?" Fallon asked.

"O'Brien was in the church early one day, and the Devil appeared, just as we imagine him to be with horns and a tail. He tried to tempt O'Brien, and didn't leave until O'Brien banished him with some cabbalistic curse."

"How did the Devil tempt him?" Elizabeth looked interested.

"It would appear that the good father had impure thoughts towards a certain young woman." There was a moment of surprised silence, and then a few smiles appeared. Crooke wagged his finger at them, "It's a serious thing to a Catholic priest, and we shouldn't treat it lightly!"

"That's easily explained!" Fallon raised both hands to his head as though to contain the thoughts there, "The Devil was a creation of O'Brien's mind, and obviously the impure thoughts caused a conflict with his vocation, and that produced a projection of the Devil."

"That sounds like a normal breakdown to me!" the sheriff shook his head slightly, "Don't get me wrong, I realise that a breakdown can be serious, and I can sympathise with anyone suffering from one."

"Ah, there's a bit more," Donovan interrupted, "I have the reports of the accident, and from the witnesses, including a patrol officer, all agree that O'Brien was driving well over a hundred and swerving like a drunk. At the same time, he was yelling and waving his fist at something in front of him. No one saw anything ahead of him that could cause this reaction."

"Was he drunk?" the sheriff asked the obvious question, and Donovan shook his head and continued, "It would appear that he deliberately drove at the tanker at full speed."

"He committed suicide, and that is a serious sin in the eyes of the church," Elizabeth seemed to be thinking aloud, "He must have had a good reason to choose that way out."

"I think that he believed that he was destroying something evil, and he chose a martyr's death," Donovan explained, and everyone was struck dumb as they thought of O'Brien's terror that was so real that he committed suicide.

"I can add a few things that were also confirmed by the archbishop," Crooke helped himself to the sheriff's coffee, "Over the years O'Brien came into the hospital as part of his clerical duties, last rites and giving comfort to patients, and we had many long conversations. He didn't believe in miracles, God, or the Devil, and he'd been that way all his life."

The sheriff looked confused, "Then why did he become a priest?"

"He thought this way," Crooke explained, "If there was no heaven or hell, no God or Devil, then good and evil must reside within us and not in the supernatural. He took up the church to help people overcome their inner demons."

Elizabeth reached out and took the coffee out of Crooke's hand, "I can imagine that you spend your whole life believing in one thing, and having that overturned must have been a shock. Imagine that you didn't believe in elephants, and then one day came face to face with one!"

"It must have seemed very real to him," Donovan at last sat down, "If the Devil appeared to him in front of the car, he may have driven at the truck in an effort to kill the apparition."

"A bit drastic!" Fallon winced, "If he had started to believe in the Devil, he may have also started to think that the anti-Christ was coming, Armageddon, and perhaps he thought of all the martyrs that gave their lives in the name of God, so his was an inevitable sacrifice."

"It could also have driven him out of his mind!" the sheriff grunted, "It would certainly have driven me nuts!"

"Are we agreed that this was an 'event'?" Elizabeth looked at them and received reluctant nods.

"There's something else we must address," Donovan rubbed his face to get the picture of the Devil out of his mind, "The gang came in to see me about the veracity of O'Brien's death, and the conversation began to veer towards the strange things that have been happening around here. I managed to steer them away from the subject, but Megan didn't seem convinced. Since the departure of Marcus, she has become the brains of the outfit, and quite capable of finding out a lot more."

"What do you want me to do, lock her up?" the sheriff smiled at the thought.

"I have thought about this, not the locking up," Elizabeth admitted, "There's no such thing as a secret, and eventually other people would start putting the facts together and asking questions."

"What do you do in such circumstances?" Cooke asked.

"In times of war, we lock them up," Elizabeth nodded to the sheriff, "but this is not wartime; we're not sure what it is!"

"Wouldn't it be better to take them into our confidence," Donovan suggested, "at least it would stop wild rumours and conspiracy theories."

"They're a tight-knit group," Elizabeth looked for confirmation, "Can we trust them to keep a lid on this for the public good?"

"The centre of the group would, that's Megan, Billy, Joel, Sean and Gerry, if Marcus comes back we can include him." Donovan ticked them off, "I'm not sure about Suzy, she was deeply upset over O'Brien's death, but she's getting in deeper with them."

"She's also been a possible victim," Elizabeth pointed out, "That could cause a conflict within her."

"The same can be said of Marcus, Gerry and Joel," Donovan argued, "I would trust them to behave themselves. They're a nucleus of reasonable behaviour in the school and most of the other youngsters."

"We also have a distraught archbishop to deal with," Crooke pointed out, "It doesn't seem fair to keep him in a state of fear about Armageddon."

Elizabeth agreed, "I'll try and have a talk to Megan by herself, and could you Crooke have a word with the archbishop, as you've already made contact. I think he'll be relieved!"

Chapter Fifty-One

Megan was surprised to find the agent walking alongside her as she made her way to the Grill after school.

"Hi! Can we have a girl to girl chat?" Elizabeth asked.

"What about? I'm just on my way to meet the boys." Megan felt uncomfortable at talking to the agent by herself. What if this is an attempt to divert her suspicions.

"That's what I want to talk about. You're pretty well in with them."

"What have they done this time?" Megan pulled a face.

"Nothing that I'm aware of, apart from under-age drinking, and if we arrested everyone who'd done that, there wouldn't be anyone left!" Elizabeth tried to put on her friendliest face, "I'm just interested, they stand out as a group."

Megan searched the agent's face for some sign of deceit, and decided there wasn't one, "They're a great bunch of guys, you've heard about their football success this year? Joel is really a gentle giant. When he started school, the other kids made fun of his size, but he ignored them, and when they started bullying him, then he retaliated, and it stopped instantly; no one bullies Joel! They started making hell for Marcus 'cos he was so skinny and bright, but Joel stopped that too. I think that was when the gang started to come together. Billy and Gerry came at the same time; I think that I remember that the three of them made some stand against the bullies."

"What about the others?"

"They don't act stupid like the other boys," Megan gave a brief laugh, "Of course they do act stupid, especially Gerry, but they don't try it on. I guess I mean that they respect people, and I feel safe in their company."

"You feel safe in their company?" Elizabeth looked and sounded surprised.

Megan nodded vigorously, "There's no safer place I would like to be. Billy's a flirt, and Gerry would like to be, but then, so am I; it's just good fun without the risks."

They came to a bench, and Elizabeth sat down, and Megan joined her after a short hesitation, "What do you really want to talk about," she asked.

Elizabeth threw her head back and looked at the sky, "I thought you were bright! You've been thinking things, such as what I'm doing here, am I right?"

"Yeah, we thought for a while that you fancied Donovan, but we couldn't see how the bureau would allow you so much time off. Then I thought that it was something to do with the weird things that have been happening."

"Donovan's a nice guy, and I wouldn't mind, strictly speaking between us girls! You're right; it's about the weird things, and I want your assurance that from this moment none of this goes any further." Elizabeth said with a stern expression.

"Even with the guys?"

"For the moment," Elizabeth had to be careful not to alienate the girl, "We're in the middle of an investigation, and we have very few answers if any, and we don't want people coming out with controversy theories or wild ideas."

"I can understand that, and we've discussed conspiracy theories," the girl nodded, "I promise to keep quiet, unless I think that you're not being straight; how's that?"

"Good enough, I can't expect more when you don't know anything," Elizabeth took a deep breath, "I run a department that you would call the X-Files." Megan's eyes opened wide, and Elizabeth continued, "It's not exactly as you've seen on TV. We pick up on anything outside of the normal day to day operations, and sometimes we catch crooks, and sometimes we catch nothing, usually nothing."

"And you picked up on the weird things happening here?" Megan began to see the light.

"Not just here, there are similar things happening across the country, and that's why we think there's something going on," Elizabeth looked over to her companion to see what effect this was making, "A little while ago everything was so vague and disjointed, my chiefs decided to close the operation down."

"It's over the whole country?" Megan looked horrified. "We thought that is was just outside the town and maybe the state."

"No, it's a wide belt from New York to Portland, and that's why we were so worried at first. We thought that something had been dropped by an aircraft or even a satellite, from the Chinese, Russians, or Muslims, or whoever, but none of the flight paths were over that area, close but not exactly. We've a scientist, what you would call a nerd, working for us who's trying to find probabilities and such."

"You mean like Numbers on TV," Megan said, "We've seen him working in Donovan's office, and I was with Marcus when he asked the nerd's advice about Princeton."

"That's the guy; he's called Demetrius. The really off-putting thing is that everyone affected acts differently, and that's why the bureau wanted to shut us down. None of it makes sense! We don't know of any single substance or concoction that makes people act in so many different ways." Elizabeth threw her hands up to demonstrate the conundrum, "Until we get a positive lead, we don't want anyone interfering."

"I get what you're saying," Megan pulled a face by twisting her mouth. "We thought that it might be a biological weapon from somewhere, but nothing made sense as you say. We were looking at old newspapers to find out what it was that kept you here. I guess we'd better stop that!"

"Yes please, but now you will know what we know, and it'll be a waste of time! How do you think the guys would react to this news?"

"No problems with that; I guess you don't want to start a panic," Megan stared at the agent, "This feels really scary; would you like to come with me and speak to the guys?"

"I feel like a coffee, so lead on!"

Chapter Fifty-Two

"How did the archbishop take it?" Elizabeth asked Crooke in his office.

"He was mightily relieved that he wouldn't be in mortal combat with Satan!" Crooke laughed, "He didn't know which way to turn, but I explained that although O'Brien's experience and probably his death fitted into the other events, it was something either natural or man-made and not supernatural. He was worried about whatever this is, and he offered help if we need it."

"At the moment, we could do with a helping hand from God!" Elizabeth sighed.

"When's Demetrius coming back?" Donovan had become accustomed to the scientist occupying his desk.

"When he's finished!" Elizabeth waved a hand, "He has no real concept of time, and when I reproached him about it ages ago, he said it was a strange variable, whatever that means!"

"Did you manage to chat with Megan?"

"Yeah and just in time! It would have been just another couple of days or weeks before they would know what we know, more or less," Elizabeth crossed her legs and made herself comfortable, "She's a bright, sensible kid; not bright like Marcus, but streetwise. She understood and was ahead of me several times. We ended up in the Grill with the gang, and they promised that they would behave themselves, especially if we keep them in the loop. Suzy was a problem; she didn't take to the idea that she had been a victim of something mysterious, but then she got angry at whatever it was and agreed not to rock the boat. The whole group offered to help if we needed extra hands. Do you know that they had all the right ideas, almost the same as ours?"

Donovan chuckled, "Without any of our resources; that's amazing!"

"Not really, it was my sudden appearance that started them questioning what was going on," Elizabeth pulled a face, "What I find incredible is that they were seriously thinking of biochemical warfare. We shouldn't under-rate them; I certainly won't!"

"Now all we want is to know what it is we're fighting!" said Crooke gloomily.

The same question was being asked on the bleachers where the gang had gathered for some privacy. No one else was on the field except for a couple of runners.

"This is really spooky!" Suzy shuddered as she expressed her feelings.

Gerry gave a devilish laugh, "They're coming to get you!"

Both Suzy and Megan punched him, "That's not funny! Suzy has already been 'got at', as you so crudely put it!" Billy just shook his head and sighed at his friend's antics.

"You should think before you speak, idiot!" Joel rumbled, "Some of us are deeply involved, and that includes you!"

Gerry was suitably contrite, "Sorry, I guess I wasn't thinking. I didn't mean anything Suzy." She punched him again to show that there was no harm done.

"We don't know who's involved," Megan stated, "We have all the efforts of the FBI to track this down, and they're stumped, and they can call on anything in the country and beyond, computers, specialists, anything!"

"What I can understand from what we've been told is that it's difficult to tell the difference between something normal and something abnormal," Billy leant back and stared at the sky, "We have people seeing things, and that's almost normal; people have funny turns all of the time. Then we have miraculous cures which could be natural and then some very strange things which aren't normal."

"None of it is normal round here!" Gerry took his sneaker off and tipped out a pebble, "My folks moved here because it wasn't like the cities; they just wanted normal, uneventful lives."

"Then they had you! That must have upset them!" Suzy got her own back.

"What can make one person nuts, and yet can cure another person?" Joel asked.

"That's why the FBI are at a loss; a single something that creates different results," Billy answered.

"What about the band across the country?" Megan said, "Do you think that someone dropped something from an aircraft?"

Billy shook his head, "That's been well covered, and it's impossible these days for an aircraft to do anything odd; if a pilot twitches, he'll have a fighter on his tail in no time. Light aircraft don't have the range to cross the country, and even they are closely observed for flight safety."

"What about something from space?" Gerry decided to act properly.

Billy shook his head again, "They track all of the space junk up there, and there's an army of observers looking for near-earth-objects, not just the major observatories but thousands of amateur astronomers. It would have been noticed by someone."

"I feel lost without Marcus!" Joel frowned.

"Can we contact him?" Suzy asked.

"He's up to his eyebrows in math," Billy said, "It wouldn't be fair to distract him, plus he may be one of the victims."

"It's Thanksgiving next week, and he said he'd be home." Megan reminded them.

"Oh yeah, I wonder if he'll have to change his hat size?" Gerry grinned, "I'll call him Mister Bighead!"

"What I don't understand is what happened to me," Suzy almost wailed, "How does taking my clothes off and running into the woods make me a victim?"

Gerry leant in towards her, "Tell me child, do you often have these compulsions, and can I be there when you do it again?"

Megan really hit him, but Suzy giggled. Gerry howled and clutched his arm where Megan had really struck him, "It was just scientific interest!" he said.

"I think that Megan and Billy should keep close to Agent Long-legs and Donovan so that we are kept up to date," Joel got up, "Here comes Ding-dong."

Sure enough, the coach was walking their way.

"I'll take the agent so that Billy won't lose concentration," Megan smiled impishly, "and he can take on Donovan."

"You just like to spoil a guy's dreams," Billy smiled back at her, "but as they are often together, it won't be much of a hardship."

Ding-dong just wanted to arrange some details for the next game which was on the day before Thanksgiving.

Chapter Fifty-Three

Marcus did make it home in time for Thanksgiving, and Megan collared him on the way to the game. She filled him in on the details, and his face changed through from interest to incredulity to intense interest. Then it turned pale.

"They really think that I have been infected?" he burst out finally.

"And probably Joel, Gerry and Suzy. We don't know who has been infected or what with," Megan stated, "all they are saying is that some people have been affected more than others, and in different ways."

"You've not been infected?" Marcus stared at her to check if she had grown another head.

"Not that they know," Megan said, and Marcus continued to stare at her intently, but said nothing. He looked thoughtful and walked backwards and forwards, muttering to himself. Eventually, he turned back to Megan, "The distribution would have to be the same as a toxic gas released from high altitude."

"Yeah, the FBI had already thought about that, but there were no aircraft or satellites flying that course for at least a year, if ever," Megan explained.

"Huh, I think we'll miss the game if we stand around any longer," Marcus took her arm, "I've waited all this time to see the gang in action again, and I can see the FBI afterwards."

Megan laughed, "Do you mean while they were cramming your head full of equations, algorithms and whatnot, all you could think of was the gang playing?"

Marcus laughed with her, "It was the only form of relief that I had, besides I hear that they are keeping up a formidable game!"

The game was well worth waiting for. Joel was charging through the opposition as usual, and passing at the right moment to Billy, Gerry or Sean. Then they changed tactics. Gerry had the ball and an opponent made a charge, and would have succeeded but for Joel. He was too far away to stop the opposing player, but not so far from Gerry, and he picked him up and clear of the tackle, and then threw Gerry over the heads of the opposing team. It was a prodigious throw, and Gerry hung on to the ball and hit the ground, performed a forward roll and came up running to pass over the line. He started doing a victory dance while the opponents, struck dumb for a moment, erupted in a roar of protest.

The spectators roared as well, and the referee screamed for attention. He couldn't remember if such a move was legal or even tried before. The opposing team captain was poking him in the chest and shouting into his face. He knocked the arm away, and in a few minutes, he could be heard.

"There is nothing in the rule book that says this is legal or illegal, and I'm going to make a ruling. I'm going to allow the score…" The teams started shouting again, and a few fights started, "I'm allowing this score, and that's final, but if it happens again, it's a foul! That's it! Get that clown back here with the ball and play on."

It didn't make much difference to the score; White Tail Butte High flattened the opposition with a final drop kick from Gerry.

"Hey man, that was awesome!" Marcus said when he and Megan met them coming out of the changing rooms.

"Hey, genius, glad to see you again!" Joel was putting on his jacket over his tee shirt, but Megan stopped him.

"What the hell is that?" she pointed.

Joel looked down at a massive bruise on his arm, "Aw, they always try to do some damage."

"You should see the rest of him!" Billy said, "He's black and blue all over!"

"Now there's a thought!" Megan's face screwed up, and she let out a cackle of wicked laughter.

"A couple of hours in a sauna and some of Dad's special lotion, and they'll be all gone!" Joel pulled on his jacket and gave Megan a hooded look.

"Jeez, I'll stick to tiddely-winks!" Marcus winced.

"How was the yooneeversity, Young Einstein?" Gerry put his arm around Marcus's shoulders and measured his head with the other hand.

"Hell, and I can't begin to explain to a moron like you!" Marcus looked happy to be teased.

"I told you everyone called you a moron," Joel pushed Gerry away and put his enormous arm across his friend's shoulder, "Good to see you, and you're just in time to solve a problem, Sherlock."

"So I've heard," Marcus looked up at the giant, "I'll have to get some more facts before making any comment."

"We've decided that only Megan and Billy should approach the FBI; it would look conspicuous if we all kept marching in there, but I suppose you'll not attract much attention," Suzy said.

"Tell us more about Princeton; what are the guys like?" Billy asked.

"They're just like us." Marcus shrugged.

"You said we were morons!" Gerry objected.

"Ah, but they are superior morons!" Marcus explained, "Honestly, they fool around just like us, even the professors. If a joke gets the message across, they'll use it, and nothing is sacred."

"That's sounds unbelievable!" Sean said, "I thought that they would walk around in silence like monks."

Marcus shook his head, "The whole point of science is to find the truth. They examine everything and keep doing so, even giants like Newton and Einstein are not treated as sacred cows."

"But when we rang you, you said that it was hard going," Billy countered.

"It is! They introduced me to ideas and concepts I'd never dreamed of, and then provided the math to go with it. I have to take a lot of aspirin!"

"You poor guy!" Gerry leant his head on Marcus in mock sympathy.

"Thanks, I appreciate your sorrow at my plight," Marcus straightened his shoulders, "Now I would like to meet the FBI agents."

"No one here," Billy informed him, "They've all gone home for Thanksgiving. There's still Crooke and Donovan around."

"It can wait a while. I've got until after Christmas to recharge my batteries," Marcus grinned again at his friends, "What are we going to do in that time?"

Gerry stated whistling and humming the theme from the Twilight Zone.

Chapter Fifty-Four

Demetrius returned just before Christmas. Donovan looked up in surprise as the door opened and the Greek mathematician dropped his bags on the floor but gently placed his briefcase on a desk.

"Hello and welcome back; where have you been?" Donovan greeted him.

"Everywhere, talking to people, reading reports, assessing photographs; I'm totally worn out!" Demetrius slumped into a chair with a sigh.

"What did you find out?"

Demetrius waved a tired hand, "Wait until I get my breath back. There is still a lot of work to do confirming my ideas, but at least I'm not doing that; I've entrusted others with the task."

"I'll get you a coffee," Donovan stood and walked to the coffee table, "Everyone else is out somewhere or other."

"Good, I'll wait until we're all here before laying out my results so far," Demetrius gulped down the hot coffee.

"The team is quite a bit larger," Donovan explained, "We had to include the gang of kids because they were getting close to the stories and we thought that bringing them in would stop wild speculations. We also had to bring in the archbishop," his face became very serious, "We lost Father O'Brien, but not before he told the archbishop that he had been talking to the Devil. O'Brien was killed soon after in a car crash, and the archbishop started to worry that it marked the Coming of the Anti-Christ."

Demetrius opened his eyes wide, "I was brought up as Greek Orthodox, and we take such matters seriously, however, it does fit into the picture."

"You're better off than any of us; the picture here is badly out of focus!" Donovan plumped down in his old office chair.

When Elizabeth returned a few days later, she was pleased to see the little Greek, but couldn't get very much out of him, and that left her with where to hold a meeting so that Demetrius could tell everyone at the same time.

"The problem is that I don't want to attract attention to the meeting because there are so many involved," she said, "and I don't want anyone overhearing."

"We also need a large monitor to present the data," Demetrius added.

"That's settled then!" the agent said firmly, "It will have to be at HQ in Portland; it has the right size, all the electronic gizmos, and it's secure!"

"I'll check on people's schedules, and I'll include the gang," Donovan reached for a 'phone, "When do you want to hold this party?"

"On Saturday, if that's okay with you Demetrius?" she asked, and the mathematician nodded.

The gang arrived at the FBI HQ in Portland in two pickups, Joel's and Billy's.

"It's a lot smaller than I thought it would be!" Gerry cranked his neck out of the window of Billy's pickup. They parked and got out, and all had the same opinion.

"Well, the sign says FBI, so I guess it is," Marcus pointed to the sign.

"Ah my Dear Watson," Gerry sucked on an imaginary pipe, "It stands for the Federation of Bald Indians; elementary!"

"Try not to clown around too much Sherlock, or they'll lock you up," Billy cautioned him.

"Or I will!" rumbled Joel, "Permanently!"

"There's your girlfriend waiting for us," Megan pointed to the door.

"Yes, she's an impatient wench!" Gerry stepped sideways to avoid Megan's swipe.

"You found us then; welcome to FBI Portland," Elizabeth had heard Gerry's remarks and was struggling to keep a straight face, "You'll have to sign in and wear ID tags."

"Just like dogs!" Gerry said brightly, "Can I be your pet poodle?"

"You've got a dog's brain!" said Billy and kicked his backside.

"Cruelty to animals!" Gerry accused him clutching his butt, "You should be more tolerant; I'm confused, one minute I'm a moron, and the next a dog!"

"We would have got here earlier, but Gerry was navigating," Joel explained.

"No one told me that the map was upside-down!" complained the navigator.

"We thought that it would be a taller building," Suzy looked round at what appeared to be a normal office foyer.

"This is just an extension," Elizabeth waved a hand, "The main office is downtown, but you're probably thinking of the place in Washington that's always on TV."

"In the X-Files, they put Mulder in the basement, but here you're even out of the main building!" Sean said, "They must be really ashamed of you!"

Elizabeth laughed, "Embarrassed would be a better word; everyone's waiting, so follow me, and it's the top floor, not the basement. What excuse did you give your parents for coming here?"

"We told them the truth – almost," Billy answered, "They knew that you were FBI or something, and we said that you'd offered to show us around."

"Clever!" Elizabeth nodded, "The closer to the truth the better."

"I told my folks that you were recruiting us as spies," Gerry added.

"And they believed you?" Elizabeth asked.

"Nah, they knew that I don't look like James Bond." Gerry hung his head in mock shame.

She led them to a lift, and then from there to a large conference room. The table had moved to one side and the chairs scattered in a haphazard and relaxed way.

"Help yourselves to coffee or OJ, and there should be some Danish. You know everyone here except Archbishop Harrison."

"So you're the young people involved in this," the archbishop shook their hands; Gerry curtsied!

At one end of the room was a large screen, and to one side of that sat Demetrius, patiently waiting to start.

"So Demetrius tell us what you have found out," Elizabeth sat and crossed her legs which attracted the attention of the boys.

"Ah my friends, I have found nothing!" The Greek scientist smiled as he announced his bombshell.

Chapter Fifty-Five

"Why the hell have you brought us here?" Fallon asked, and then looked at the archbishop, "Sorry!"

"No problem, I had a similar phrase come to mind," the archbishop said with a slight smile.

"I don't think that Demetrius would waste our time," Elizabeth said as she settled back in her chair. She had become accustomed to the way he worked.

"I have not found what you call a smoking gun," Demetrius didn't look at all put out by Fallon's outburst, "No gun, but an awful lot of smoke!"

"You mean that you've found out a lot of clues, the smoke, but you're not sure what made it," Marcus said.

"Precisely, and at the moment none of it can be proved, but some reliable people are working on it."

Elizabeth looked worried, "I hope that they do not know the full story?"

Demetrius shook his head, "I separated out the tasks so that no one can understand the true meaning."

"Okay Demetrius, don't keep us in suspense," Elizabeth urged her pet scientist.

Demetrius shrugged his shoulders, "It's not that simple, and I'll have to lead you through step by step. We have established that something happened probably in the spring or early summer, but we were not aware of it until the start of the summer holidays."

"When we went camping," Billy said.

Demetrius nodded, "You and a few thousand others. Correct me if I'm wrong Elizabeth, but have the events slowed down or stopped?"

Elizabeth nodded, "All we're picking up now is past events."

"People are more active in the summer, and this may also indicate that the agent that caused this is also only active in the warm summer days, or maybe both or one. Tell me, what is the difference between town and country?"

"More people in towns," Billy thought aloud, "more traffic and less grass."

"And more concrete! Every day the concrete is washed, clearing all of the dirt away. Whatever this is, it prefers to be in nature, and then we come to you young people."

The gang looked at one another and then back to Demetrius, "Yes, you boys are a fine indicator of what is going on. Here is a graph of you all recording your academic progress over the last five years. I took them from the school records." Demetrius tapped on the laptop, and a graph appeared on the screen.

"This is a record of your yearly marks, but look what has happened this year," Demetrius pointed to the right side of the screen, and everyone made a muttered comment. "You see that for four years there was a steady progression, but this year there is a sharp upwards movement."

"You would expect that with children," the archbishop said.

"Yes and I agree, but look at the Marcus line, it almost goes vertical," Demetrius pointed.

"Gee man, it looks like a NASA rocket!" Gerry gasped.

"I'll show now how the boys played football based on their scores." Another graph flashed onto the screen, "You can see here that there is a steady progression until the last year, and all show that same break upwards, especially Joel and Gerry with Billy and Sean just trailing behind."

"I still can't see that it's anything particularly different to any other kid's development," Fallon looked increasingly puzzled.

Demetrius wagged a finger at Fallon, "Please remember what you have just said; it's vitally important! I also went to some schools way outside of the Zone, the belt across the country, and these are the results."

There was a quiet hush as everyone studied the charts.

"There's no kick-up at the end!" Elizabeth observed.

"These are some of the graphs from schools within the Zone," Demetrius showed another series of graphs. "You will notice that all have that kick-up as you call it; some more pronounced than others."

"Are there any individuals that have developed like Joel and Marcus?" Crooke asked.

"Yes, and in many different ways," Demetrius confirmed, "some of the developments are difficult to quantify and can't be placed on a graph; things like art, literature, languages and even social interactions."

"I'm no scientist by any stretch of the imagination," the archbishop said, "but I can see that there has been a dramatic increase and that it is unnatural."

"This presents something I can give to my chiefs to prove something happened, and that I haven't been totally wasting my time," Elizabeth frowned at the screen, "but what has caused this?"

The little scientist smiled, "Ah yes, that has been the puzzle from the beginning, how did this agent arrive and what is it? I shall try to answer that, but it is only conjecture for the time being, and may remain that way for some years to come."

He tapped at the laptop again, and a new diagram appeared, "This is the story of evolution, Darwin's famous theory. Are you comfortable with this concept Archbishop?"

"The church has long accepted that the Bible's version of Creation is just a guide line, and just as unreliable as any other theory, simply because no one was there at the time," the archbishop replied.

"Good, at least we are on the same footing," Demetrius smiled at the priest, "I was talking to the Vatican's science officer recently on this point and others, and he said the same thing, but there is always room for individual beliefs. In science, we are always changing our minds."

"Does this have something to do with evolution?" Marcus asked.

"Yes it does, but it is only one explanation," Demetrius turned to the screen, "You will notice that the story of life on this planet is divided into sections. The first two epochs, the Hadean and Archaean are when the planet evolved geologically, but there is evidence that life of sorts started in the Archaean. I won't bother with all of the details, although they are in my report, but there is evidence that life started very early, and was made extinct many times by geological activity and meteor bombardment."

"The Ancient Greeks believed that the world was created out of chaos," the archbishop said, "Your description appears to agree with that."

"I'm obviously well aware of the beliefs of my ancestors," Demetrius smiled, "but in this case, they would have been very accurate, but the meteors would have added to the bulk of the planet and brought water; so important to the existence of life. I'm not going to go into the different arguments about how life started; we'll have to be content with the fact that it did. On the left of the line are the epochs and on the right you will see other markers. These denote a rapid biological change and a mystery almost as great as the creation of life itself."

"I thought that meteors caused extinctions," Fallon said.

"You're thinking of the Dinosaur extinction that made the rise of mammals possible, but I'm thinking of something more subtle. Why did little microbes decide that they would become complex creatures? Why did plants move from being seaweed to grass and then bushes and trees? Why did some plants choose to grow

267

seeds, and some nuts, and others fruit? These things happened over an incredibly short time. What was the trigger?"

"Darwin's theory says that certain animal features changed as the climate and environment changed," Crooke said, "That was the trigger!"

"You're talking about the Cambrian explosion!" Marcus had kept quiet until now but now showed that he was keeping up with the argument.

"That is a major feature here," Demetrius became excited, "Pre-Cambrian Earth was a rather dull place, muddy, noxious and unpleasant; then all types of creatures and plants appeared on land and in the seas." Demetrius stood and went to fetch himself an OJ.

"Couldn't that be caused by meteors or volcanoes?" Fallon asked.

"I thought that it was an increase in oxygen that created the Cambrian explosion!" Marcus said.

"True, it could have been, but how and why did the creatures increase oxygen output? They did that, but there was a sound reason. Let me set a different scenario for you," Demetrius took a long gulp of juice, "As the ice fields receded at the end of the last ice age, the Mammoth kept its woolly fur and followed the ice. Some stayed where they were and lost the fur to become Elephants. Despite the ice always being within reach, the Mammoth expired. What made the Elephant stay and why did the Mammoth have to move? One would think that all of the pachyderms would have done the same thing!"

Everyone thought about the question, looking at each other for inspiration.

"We don't know," Billy said eventually, "give up, what's the answer?"

Demetrius lifted his shoulders, "I don't know either; I wasn't there!"

Crooke started laughing, "Where are you going with this? I have a feeling that you want us to provide the answer."

"To some extent you are correct, but it's just to get your minds working to accept what I will reveal later. I'll give you another scenario," Demetrius sat down, "Hominids have been around for several million years or more, and there are just a few of the great apes left; we're one and the others are the Gorillas, Orangutan and the Chimpanzees. We all have opposable thumbs, in fact, they have four, two on their feet. Of the four groups, three live in communities, but not the Orangutan, despite the fact that they are very sociable, even when they meet us. Why? Why also is it that just we, the humans have developed a high technology and a complex language? We are so close genetically to the others, especially the Chimpanzees, that there is no obvious reason that we should be so different. In the past there were other hominids, but they didn't survive, and in very recent times we have the case of the Neanderthal; they were almost identical to us, they had fire and tools and should have survived, but they didn't."

"Is this where you have been for a few months?" Elizabeth joined in, "You've been talking to anthropologists and archaeologists."

"I had to get my facts correct," Demetrius apologised, "and I've been to others as well. It's a complex question."

Donovan had been listening intently, his legs pushed out and crossed, "I can't see that this differs very much from Darwin's theories; creatures evolve, and some die out."

"It differs very little, that's what I meant when I said it was subtle," Demetrius locked his hands together; "it's the mechanism that makes the difference!"

"I still don't see it!" said Donovan and others murmured agreement.

"We can pause for a moment and move on to the Zone, and where it came from, maybe it will help you to understand," Demetrius turned back to the screen but was stopped by Megan.

"You haven't said anything about Suzy! Does she fit into this and how?"

Demetrius turned slowly round to face her, "At last, I've been waiting for someone to ask!"

"I was waiting for you to say something!" Megan fired back.

Demetrius tapped the keys of the laptop, and a new graph appeared with just two lines, "The top line is Megan, and the bottom one is Suzy; please notice the kink in the last year."

"But that's impossible!" Megan cried out, "Neither of us were on that camping trip!"

Demetrius slowly nodded, "Interesting, is it not?"

"Now wait a minute!" Crooke pointed angrily at the screen, "We thought that the agent was in the forests and parks, but if the girls have been affected, it means that it's everywhere and there must be more victims! We are all infected!"

"You are correct!" Demetrius finally released the bombshell!

Chapter Fifty-Six

They caused such a commotion that office doors opened down the corridor and people wondered what had happened. Eventually, Elizabeth managed to be heard and calmed them down.

"This is only a theory, so sit back down and listen to the rest!"

"The doctor is correct, but there is a strong likelihood that you have all been infected, but listen to what that would mean before panicking," Demetrius waved them back to their seats. Only Billy, Marcus and Megan had not moved.

As they took their seat, Demetrius put things into perspective, "None of you have been seeing strange creatures or doing strange things, so please keep your cool until you hear everything."

"Suzy and Marcus have been doing strange things!" Megan said quietly, "very strange things!

"We should hear everything, in any case," Elizabeth sat down.

"And now Billy and me!" Megan obviously was upset.

"I said that we should look at the Zone, but before that, I want to show you what happened to people living outside of the Zone, but travelled into it during this period." Demetrius produced another graph, "These people were infected when they entered the Zone or showed symptoms, so I took readings of the schools in those areas. As you can see, there is no sign of a kink in any of these schools." A series of graphs rapidly flowed across the screen.

"That means that the infection or agent does not pass from an individual by touch or by air," Crooke looked thoughtful, "It has to be directly from agent to subject, and possibly only during warm weather."

"That's what my colleagues and I think as well," Demetrius said.

"Does that mean we are infected or not?" Donovan looked uncertain.

"Maybe not, but most probably you are but, and please listen!" Demetrius held his hand up to quell any further outbursts, "but we do not know the nature of this agent, or how it affects people. There may be no risk even if you are infected!"

"Can you tell us how the Zone was created?" Marcus asked, but his tone suggested that he knew.

Demetrius positively beamed, "Your stay at Princeton has made its mark! It was not by an aircraft or a chunk of a satellite; it was a meteor!"

"Now I get it!" Marcus lurched forward so fast his glasses flew off his nose, "Transpermia, that's what you were leading up to! Those rapid changes in evolution were caused by meteors, and in the case of apes and humans, only a part of the animal world was affected, not every ape!"

"Well done! Yes we have long thought that some meteors, a few may carry organic material that we call endospores." Demetrius looked as excited as Marcus, "when they hit the atmosphere the outer material burns away during deceleration, and then the dust which was protected from the heat and containing the organic stuff floats down to the surface."

"So why the strange behaviour?" Fallon didn't look convinced, and Marcus tried to explain.

"Its different behaviour all of the time; very few events are alike because we are different to each other, our DNA is different, and our fingerprints, and we're wired differently."

"That's a very good way to put it," Demetrius clapped his hands softly, "We are chemical factories, every living thing on the planet and our chemicals vary. If you think of an outbreak of influenza, most people will react in almost the same way, but some will die, and others may suffer nothing more than a sniffle – and some will not be affected at all!"

"This is slightly more than just a head cold!" Fallon said sarcastically, "I still don't believe that this came from outer space."

"Yes Mister Fallon, that is obvious, but we know quite a lot more about it now," Demetrius replied, "I did consider that this is a man-made virus, perhaps something that went wrong, but the delivery, the creation of the Zone excludes that!"

"That's why you gave us a lecture about evolution," Megan said.

The Greek nodded sombrely, "What I didn't explain then was why there is such a thing as evolution."

"I thought it was all about survival of the species," Elizabeth said.

"Survival yes, but not necessarily of a species," Demetrius folded his hands over his stomach, "if that were the case, we would not have progressed beyond a single-celled creature. What pushes evolution is the changing environment, but it needs the added factor of the agent. We could not have lived in the conditions that existed four billion years ago, but as the environment changed, the simple and then multi-celled creature adapted until you see what we have today. For approximately twenty to fifty thousand years, and there are indications that it was much longer, humans have created civilisation, an artificial environment which has helped us to dominate the natural world."

"We had a talk about this in Princeton," Marcus interrupted, "In the past, as nature changed we had to adapt to the changes, but now we make the world to suit us, and the need for evolution has diminished."

"I see that your time really has not been wasted," Demetrius paused, "Evolution is a force of nature and cannot be stopped, but it can be diverted. Civilisation has blocked one avenue, and that has led some commentators to say that we have reached the ultimate goal of development, but we are changing our environment, we are reaching out to other worlds, both physically and intellectually and nature, evolution has to respond."

"Where does a meteor come into this?" Fallon still failed to make a connection.

Joel surprised everyone by speaking out in his bass voice, "I get it! Conditions change slowly, and evolution makes minute changes to keep pace, but eventually a meteor drops something that accelerates development, and the process starts all over again."

"Jeez Bro, did you go to Princeton too?" Gerry gaped up at his giant friend.

"I just listen to what's being said," Joel's paw patted Gerry on the head.

"So what is this agent?" Elizabeth asked.

"I think that it is the same thing that started life in the first place." Demetrius pushed his hair back from his eyes, "Consider that there is an ocean of chemical soup where life started, we have produced that soup in countless variations in laboratories, and it remains as soup whatever we try. Along comes the meteor with the agent, it may be just another ingredient or it may have evolved in deep space and then frozen for millions of years in hibernation. It hits our atmosphere, heats up and breaks apart, and the agent awakes and drifts down to become part of the soup."

"Creating a life energy," Marcus whispered, seeing in his mind the events unfold.

Demetrius nodded vigorously, "The cells that are created go through various stages until another meteor arrives carrying the same agent, just as Joel said. This time it reacts slightly differently. Some cells are more successful than others at some things, such as producing oxygen, and the agent improves that ability and that creates complex cells. Each time an agent carrying meteor arrives, there is a dramatic change."

Fallon still looked doubtful, "Meteors are entering our atmosphere by the thousand every day, so why don't we see changes all the time, why do we wait for thousands and millions of years?"

Demetrius lifted his hands, "Who says that we do not?"

"We could detect those changes," Fallon continued.

"Not necessarily," Marcus had a faraway look on his face, "it's like an update on a computer program. We still see the original programme, and it appears the same, but works better. If the agent is the same or similar to the original, we couldn't detect it."

"And the original would be part of what makes us and everything else and may be in plain sight, but accepted as a basic part of everything," Megan said.

"Hey, has everyone else been to Princeton except me?" Gerry complained.

"Do you know where meteors come from?" Demetrius asked Fallon, but continued with the answer, "Ninety percent of meteors are remnants of old comets. As the comet nears the sun all of the volatiles, including water boil away and the comet breaks up. The meteor's heart still contains remnants of the original comet and follows the comet's orbit, and some of those orbits can take thousands and millions of years. That's why it arrives here only after it has completed a long journey and it may be just one particular comet we are dealing with, but I think that it is many."

"What about the different reactions to the agent?" Fallon continued being sceptical.

"I said that in the beginning, the agent improved on what the cell was already doing." Demetrius was using his hands in trying to describe his thoughts, "Look at our football team and their success, look at Marcus and the little boy who stopped being autistic."

"What about me?" Suzy interrupted.

"Ah, yes, well I've given that some thought," Demetrius placed his forefinger over his lips, "You are slightly younger than the others here, and I believe that it had something to do with puberty. The exact mechanics of the agent are difficult to understand, but it improves whatever stage you are at. You were coming of childbearing age, but probably not as advanced as Megan. I can best explain by mentioning the other cases. The old drunk..."

"Hamish!" Donovan supplied.

"Yes, Old Hamish did one thing superbly, and that was drinking himself to death; the agent accelerated that by introducing a change that his abused organs could not accept. It would appear that the agent affects the nervous system and the brain, and that would explain the man who saw dinosaurs; he had just taken his family to see a dinosaur exhibition. The man who thought he was fighting Arabs in the Middle East had been doing that a few years earlier, and his occupation at the time was as a security driver, which meant that he hadn't really changed occupation, and something threw him back a few years,"

Demetrius looked around, "This agent has two sides, on one it produce Marcus and Joel and cure diseases and the other will kill those who are evolving in the wrong direction, simply by exaggerating certain traits."

"I still don't believe that meteors cause this!" Fallon folded his arms over his chest.

"Consider it this way," Demetrius continued arguing, "A man digs a hole, a trench in the ground. He then mixes ground rock and sand with water and lays that product in the bottom of a trench. His next action is to mix clay and straw and bakes them into blocks. These blocks he lays one by one in the bottom of the trench, fixing them in place with a version of the first product. He then lays another line of blocks on top of the first, and this is repeated many times until he has built a wall."

"I get it!" Billy sat up straight, "If you didn't know what a wall was, the trench, cement, bricks and mortar would have meant very little until the wall was built."

"Quite right! This is not dealing with the bricks and mortar alone," Demetrius agreed, "There is an earlier stage of the different rocks and earlier still, the chemicals and even atoms that made up those things. If you could see an atom of carbon or hydrogen, you would not instantly connect them to the completed wall, and furthermore, those atoms can be used as the basis for many different things."

"I find it hard to believe, but I'll accept that this is possible," Fallon said, "I find the hardest thing to understand is that it can create miraculous cures and also kills."

Chapter Fifty-Seven

"I think that we should stop at that sobering point," Elizabeth stood up, "We need to think about what has been said, but I would like to know why you are so certain that it was a meteor."

"I've seen it!" Demetrius surprised them, "or rather I've seen a photograph of it. There are thousands of professional and amateur astronomers watching the skies, and they record everything on film. I guessed at roughly when this was which reduced the number of photographs to study, but it took most of the time I was away. This one was on the correct course at the right time, and broke apart over the exact part of the country."

"You've found clues and stitched them together to make a convincing argument, but it still is only a theory!" Elizabeth placed a hand on the scientist's shoulder, "It's enough to justify the effort and money I've expended, and it will create a few arguments in various circles for years to come."

"I would expect nothing less, and there will be tremendous resistance," Demetrius said as he closed the laptop, "This is as controversial as Darwin's original theory!"

Crooke nodded, "That caused a great commotion at the time, and still creates problems today."

"You guys have a long journey back," Elizabeth turned to the gang, "Fallon will show you round before you go and show some hospitality. Thanks for coming guys!"

Fallon showed the gang around the facility, almost dragging Marcus away from the laboratories and computer room. They ended up in the canteen for refreshment before leaving for home.

Elizabeth stayed talking to Demetrius, Crooke, the archbishop and Donovan. Tracy Young was present but had stayed strangely quiet all the time.

"I stopped it there because I didn't want the children to hear where the conversation was going," Elizabeth said.

"I don't think it will stop them," Demetrius shook his head, "You saw how Marcus, Megan, and a surprising Joel could follow what I was saying."

"Yeah, what about that big guy," Elizabeth agreed, "however, we left off with this agent being deadly. Would you like to explain further?"

Demetrius thought for a moment, "It's all to do with these mass extinctions that happened in the past. Some, like the one that killed off the dinosaurs, were natural disasters, but we then come to the ones that removed the early primates including the Neanderthals. It could mean that the ones that were not removed, such as Cro-Magnon were better able to compete against the Neanderthals, or whoever, who petered out for lack of resources, but much more deadly is that the agent caused their demise, and from what we have seen here, that is the most likely cause."

"Are you telling me that the agent can choose who shall live and who shall die?" Elizabeth sounded indignant.

"That is too crudely put," Demetrius replied, "No, the latest research has shown that the Neanderthal gene was also developed and many of us are descended from them. The agent is blind as to what is happening and cannot choose. When it first appeared it made things happen, some were good, and some were bad, and the bad ones didn't survive. We know of many examples where this happened; if a creature is born today with two heads, there is very little chance of it surviving, but at some time or other a cow had been provided with four stomachs and it fits into the scheme of things."

"What about the autistic boy and the old lady with dementia?" Crooke asked.

"That's what I mean when I say that the agent is blind; something happens that it has no control over, and in those two cases their brains were rewired," Demetrius said.

Tracy broke in for the first time, "We have people who died and some that have been improved; what about the majority where nothing has happened?"

"Something has happened, but it may make no real difference to their lives!" Demetrius looked from one to the other, "Some, if not all of these agents will be accepted into a host, such as ourselves, and some will be rejected. Those that remain may do nothing until another agent appears, and that may be many generations down the line."

"What do we do about this agent?" Elizabeth asked.

"Nothing!" Demetrius took her by the arm, "You don't yet appear to understand what we have here. It may have first arrived on this planet when it was forming, or at least soon after, and that started life as we know it. Subsequent arrivals kept changing that life form into what we have today, and during that process, the environment changed, and only those that could exist in the new environment survived. It's an essential part of us, and it can't be removed unless we all revert to single-celled creatures. Darwin called it the survival of the fittest; I call it The Genesis Bug."

Elizabeth, Crooke, Donovan and Tracy looked open mouthed at the little Greek scientist and then at each other.

"That's a hell of a headline!" Donovan managed to croak.

"What about my reaction to the babies?" Elizabeth asked, but her tone suggested that she didn't know if she wanted to hear the answer.

"Ah, yes our resident event," the Greek looked serious, "I don't know my dear! If you were in the Zone at the right time, you are most certainly affected. Why you reacted that way I cannot say; we are all different, and it has altered you to repeat the experiences of the mothers. We cannot tell exactly how the agent will alter us as individuals, but I have a theory of what you saw."

"I thought that you would have!" Donovan said.

"The fall into a black pit or pool with flashing lights?" Elizabeth folded her arms to suppress a shiver.

"It is a fanciful thought of mine, and a little romantic without basis of fact. It was a memory of a journey!" Demetrius paused to let that soak in, "Think of where the meteor has been, in deep space. Would not that appear as a deep black pool and the flashing lights were the stars!"

There was a momentary pause for thought, and then Donovan remembered, "That's not that different from what Timmy the autistic kid said!"

Elizabeth looked puzzled, "What does that mean?"

"I think that it's a memory of the agent's journey through space!" Demetrius stunned them into silence for a moment.

"Are you saying that this bug is aware of what is happening around it, and can remember every detail?" The Archbishop had managed to keep up with the discussion.

"It must be aware of its surroundings so that it can infest the host!" Demetrius nodded.

Chapter Fifty-Eight

"That was just getting interesting, "Billy said when they had all gathered back home in Joel's cellar. His father was out, and they wouldn't be disturbed among the tools and half-forgotten furniture.

"She stopped the meeting and threw us out!" Megan looked annoyed.

"It was getting serious, perhaps she didn't want us to hear anymore," Suzy guessed.

"Perhaps she wanted to think about what she'd heard." Marcus sat on a high bench so that he was eye to eye with Joel, "It's an incredible discovery, equal I would imagine to Darwin's theory or even DNA and she would need time to sort it out in her mind, and how she'll report it."

"I think that it's creepy!" Megan hugged herself and shivered, "Something comes from space and invades our bodies."

"The Invasion of the Body Snatchers!" Gerry pulled a series of strange faces.

"You missed the point that it made our bodies in the first place!" Marcus reminded everyone.

"That's the part that I find hard to swallow," Joel rumbled.

"It does explain why we are all different," Billy said thoughtfully, "Why does our DNA make minute differences, even between twins?"

"You think that my differences are minute? Thanks!" Joel broke out in a deep chuckle and flexed his biceps.

"Rather than thinking of body snatchers, think of them as the body makers," Billy suggested.

"I've just had a funny thought!" Sean had been quiet the whole time, but now produced something that made even Gerry stop and think, "This agent originally started all life, animals, birds, insects and fish, but didn't it also start plants. I understand that there is plant DNA and if this came down and landed everywhere, shouldn't it have affected plants as well?"

Marcus blinked, how could he have missed something so obvious? "Yes, it should have, and the birds, insects and fish."

"We've been concentrating on us little humans and forgot the rest of the world!" said Megan, "How conceited we are!"

"Worse than that," Suzy looked chastened, "we've been thinking of just us as individuals, at least I have. What happened to me was nothing; a bit embarrassing and it caused my parents an anxious moment, but in the scheme of things it was nothing."

"I've been in a bit of a dream," Marcus patted her hand, "I always wanted to go to university, but I thought that it would be too expensive; I never thought that I would be invited, and certainly not to Princeton! I too am guilty of not thinking of others."

"What did we learn?" Billy didn't like this self-reproaching and changed the subject.

"More to the point, what didn't we learn, and what can we do now?" Joel agreed with Billy.

"Yeah, we were tossed out as soon as Demetrius mentioned death," Megan realised why Billy was diverting their thoughts.

"He said that it could kill and cure," Sean said,

"Yeah, insulin is a good example of that sort of thing," Marcus nodded, "if you have diabetes insulin helps, but to a normal person, it's a deadly poison. It's also something that occurs naturally in the body."

"That's what that guy said," Gerry waved his hands excitedly; "it's something that is normally part of us."

"It's a bit more than that," Billy said. "It would appear to have a brief active life, and after it does what is does, it disappears."

Marcus shook his head, "No, it blends in! It has the perfect camouflage!"

"We've forgotten a few other things that he said such as extinction," Suzy whispered.

"That's a bit of a bummer!" Joel growled.

"I can't see how one thing can make a genius, kill somebody else, cure a disease, or make somebody see dinosaurs and Suzy to take her clothes off!" Gerry flopped in an old armchair.

"Most of those are concerned with the mind," Megan looked thoughtful, "What if this agent as Demetrius calls it, only affects the mind?"

"What about the team's success?" Billy argued, "Surely that's physical!"

"Is it?" Megan pointed to Joel who looked surprised, "He has always attacked the other team like a bulldozer, but eventually he lost the ball. Now, in recent games, just at the crucial moment, he passes to one of you who is least guarded. I've noticed that Joel doesn't look before passing – he knows! Gerry has developed a wonderful drop-kick which he could always do, but now he's one hundred percent accurate. Billy and Sean were always good at running with the ball, but now you anticipate the opponent's move much earlier. To me, that points to better mental skills!"

"She's right!" Marcus murmured, "You're good athletes, but now your brains are controlling your bodies better."

"I can't see that killing anyone!" Billy objected, "If anything I would expect an improvement and not kicking the bucket!"

"But alcoholism and drug addiction are diseases of the mind," Marcus pointed out, "Maybe there are some events where the addiction has stopped, but otherwise there is only one way out."

"It's as though you fit into the general scheme of things, or otherwise don't fit in at all!" Megan said.

"That's about the size of it!" Marcus agreed, "As far as the human race is concerned, it's a long term improvement, but a catastrophe for some individuals!"

"Even Gerry fits in, and that's really mind-boggling!" Joel said. Gerry's answer was muffled by Joel's hand over his face.

"What about the plants and animals?" Suzy asked, "I know that animals have minds, but plants don't, do they?"

"All living things have DNA and RNA, they're the basis of life," Marcus sucked his lip, "The agent could modify the DNA sequence somehow, so even if plants don't have minds, their DNA will be altered."

"I think that next time I'm in the woods, I'm going to pay particular attention to the plants around me!" Suzy said, "I saw a film the other week about things called Triffids, and I don't want to meet them, even with my clothes on!"

"There could be worse things than Triffids out there," Billy said, "I'd keep completely out of the woods if I were you."

Chapter Fifty-Nine

A bitter wind blew down Main Street as Donovan locked his office door. Thankfully, it was not snowing, but the going was slippery on a thin white film. He pulled up his collar and headed over the road to the Barbed Wire Grill, and entered the warm interior with a sigh, and promised himself for the millionth time to retire to Florida.

A party at the far end were still celebrating the New Year, creating some noise, but not objectionable. At the table near the window, Elizabeth and Demetrius were already seated, and Crooke came a few minutes later.

"I invited the sheriff, but he's doing his duty somewhere," Elizabeth said as they ordered drinks, "This marks the end of my investigation, and I wanted to thank you for your efforts. Demetrius has completed the report, and I'll hand it to my boss in a couple of days after I've read it; heaven knows what he'll think of it!"

"He won't believe it!" Demetrius said with a smile hovering at the corners of his mouth.

"I don't believe it either," Crooke said, "I've seen and heard things that I thought were impossible!"

"It's not my problem what he believes!" Elizabeth chuckled, "I'm just a G-man who reports the facts, just the facts."

"A lot of the report isn't just facts; it's an interpretation of what those facts mean," Demetrius studied the menu, "That is why I think there will be a lot of argument over the report, and I expect that it will be just filed in a dusty box."

"Don't tell us that you don't believe it either!" Donovan exclaimed.

Demetrius looked up, "I believe a lot more than I wrote, but it won't save the report."

"Why do you say that?" Donovan asked.

"Human nature is a peculiar thing," the scientist laid down his menu, "We have to believe in a certain reality. My ancestors believed that this planet was the whole of creation and that belief persisted for a very long time, some still believe that! Any deviation from a set belief will be fought to the bitter end."

The waitress interrupted and they gave their orders and replenished the drinks.

Crooke continued the discussion, "That's certainly true about Darwin; he was reluctant to publish until Wallace forced him, and the row still goes on today."

Demetrius nodded, "He's a good example. His mind was already adapted to receive new ideas by the influence of his grandfather Erasmus. I often wonder if Darwin would have come to his conclusions without that influence."

"Who and what was Erasmus?" Elizabeth asked.

"Erasmus was a very successful medical doctor in Derbyshire, England, and a keen amateur botanist, he published several books. The family married into the Wedgewood family, the famous pottery manufacturers; that gives you some idea of how successful Erasmus became. They were also close friends to the early British industrialists, and they provided an atmosphere of change."

The waitress returned with their meals, and there was the usual sorting out of which meal went where. They resumed talking after she left.

"Our report has redefined Darwin's theory, and we haven't fully accepted his original as yet," Crooke observed.

"Theories are always being redefined, sometimes by the person who came up with the theory in the first place." Demetrius looked at his plate but seemed not to see it, "The problem here is that most people think that evolution stopped when apes became humans, but evolution doesn't stop; the universe is still evolving as we sit here. Trying to get people to accept that will be the biggest problem of all."

"I'm one of those who has problems accepting change," Elizabeth said, "I haven't noticed any great change for at least a few thousand years."

"Do you remember that Joel said that evolution carries on in small ways until the agent appears?" Demetrius still hadn't started eating. "There have been slight changes that are hardly noticed. During the history of civilisation, there have been some groups that reared cattle, and others did not and this was important for their survival, for not only could they, as a last resort, eat the animal, but while it was alive, they could drink its milk and get through hard times. Today there are people who didn't rear cattle and are lactose intolerant and cannot digest milk. That is just one example."

"That's evolution?" Elizabeth sat with a puzzled expression.

Demetrius smiled at her bewilderment, "When you ask people what is Darwin's theory, they usually answer that it is the survival of the fittest. They interpret that as the strongest or fastest, but that is only part of the answer. Darwin actually said that evolution was the creature that could best adapt to changing conditions, like his finches that changed beaks to eat different food." That reminded him where they were, and he picked up his knife and fork.

"I remember you saying that nature changed and pushed evolution along," Elizabeth had stopped eating, "You also said that we had controlled nature to such an extent that it has slowed or stopped our evolution."

"We can't control nature," Demetrius said round a mouthful of food, "I said that we have set up our own environment, and that has slowed our development. We have made it possible to live longer by providing better accommodation, better food and better medication, and that has produced its own problems."

"You mean that we have set up an artificial environment inside an existing natural environment," Donovan tried to clarify the scientist's statement; "The larger and natural environment still ticks away, and will eventually alter the artificial environment."

"We have tried to play at being God, and we are only now starting to see that we're not very good at it." Demetrius nodded, "We have no way to stop earthquakes, tsunamis, drought or disease, or even the solar wind, in fact, because of our interference we cause many more problems!"

"You're thinking of global warming," Elizabeth guessed.

"I think that Demetrius is thinking of something more subtle," Donovan said, "I read somewhere that when we build a dam and create a large lake, it can alter the weather systems. A few years ago a guy did a computer simulation of weather patterns where he created or removed features such as lakes and mountains; it made huge differences in the weather."

Demetrius swallowed a mouthful of food, "We can add to that the large cities that consume huge amounts of resources and create heat and pollution. Inside our little habitations, we are changing the world around us, and that will drive evolution!"

"In what way will we evolve?" Elizabeth had lost her appetite completely.

The scientist sat back in his chair and chewed before answering, "I suspect that a lot will die. Because of our numbers and our ability to travel quickly, diseases spread very quickly, and many of those diseases are becoming resistant to medicine. Another alternative or it could happen at the same time is famine."

"It sounds like the Four Horsemen of the Apocalypse!" Elizabeth commented, "How do we combat this agent?"

"It's very apt that you choose a line from the Bible," Demetrius replied, "The Four Horsemen were the most devastating things that could happen to any community at that time as they had no answer – and in reality we still do not!"

Crooke had stopped eating and laid his knife and fork down. He hit his forehead with the heel of his hand and looked at the others with a mixture of concern and surprise, "I'm an idiot! If this interstellar agent is true and affects all forms of life, that would also include bacteria and viruses!"

"Of course it will! I thought that I made that obvious!" Demetrius looked surprised, "I do apologies for the misunderstanding."

Elizabeth's face was ashen, "I hope that you're wrong about this! Did you make it clear in the report?"

"I'm sure that I have, but we can check before it is submitted," Demetrius looked concerned, "It is only a theory, but I did mention in the report several examples, such as Bubonic Plague. It originated in Mongolia, which still remains one of the less frequented parts of the world. It left that country after the Portuguese, and Spanish trading ships started venturing there and turned up in Italian and other Mediterranean ports; from there it swept over Europe. It occurred to me that it was similar to our investigation in that it appeared only in one part of the world, and would have stayed there if it were not for the modern sailing ships, the aircraft."

Donovan held his hands up, "Let's not panic too soon! From what you have said, not all of the events are harmful," he looked to the scientist for confirmation.

"That's true, as far as the events that we have uncovered, it is under five percent have caused a change," Demetrius thought for a moment, "If we consider that there may be events we have not uncovered, we could say perhaps ten percent."

"So it's a ninety to ten chance that nothing unusual will happen," Donovan continued, "How many of that ten percent were actually beneficial, half or a quarter?"

"Oh, a lot less than that," Demetrius puckered his brow as he calculated, "I suppose that only one percent of the total caused any serious harm, probably less."

"We know that it doesn't spread like a virus," the reporter said, "It only has a limited active life, and what has happened will not cause a pandemic."

"Yes, that is true except that if it has affected a virus, which will spread!" Crooke said emphatically, "All we can do is to keep an eye on infectious diseases and be ready to act."

"This is all speculation," Demetrius restarted eating, "The agent may or may not infect anyone, and the majority of those it does will never know it, human or bug!"

Elizabeth still looked ashen, "I'm not assured that nothing will happen. I'll have to issue a warning to clinics and hospitals to be on the lookout for new strains of infections."

"It could be something not like that at all," Crooke pushed his plate away uneaten, "Do you remember those kids with minute umbilicals? Well, I checked on them this morning, and everyone is walking and talking – and I don't mean baby talk!"

"Already!" Elizabeth looked amazed, "They can't be more than a few months old!"

"Then it's started!" Demetrius stopped eating again and pushed his plate away; obviously, he had lost his appetite, "I didn't expect to see results so quickly."

Elizabeth looked accusingly at him, "What's started?" and she also felt her appetite starting to disappear.

"The next extinction! We have become like the Neanderthal, superseded by a new super race!" Demetrius didn't look shocked or surprised.

"How do you make that out?" she demanded.

"They developed further when in the womb than normal children," Demetrius reminded her, "Now they are developing physically and mentally faster than any other child."

"We can keep an eye on them!" Elizabeth tightened her lips, "How do you make out that they're a super race? The last guy who thought something like that came to a sticky end!"

"I was expecting something like this." Demetrius seemed to be lost in his thoughts, "The improvements we've seen in Marcus, Joel and the others was only an interim stage; they were already established organisms, and improvements could only go so far, but the infants were not established, they were forming in the womb. I also suspect that it will be their offspring that will bring the greater changes. You may not realise this, but Homo sapiens is about as intelligent as it can get for physical reasons that I won't go into just now. To increase intelligence would mean starting again with a radically new design of the brain and nervous system; that I believe may have happened to the new infants!"

"I thought that an increase in intelligence would lead to bigger brains," Donovan said.

"I know something of this," Crooke replied, "A larger brain would be slower as the distances the signals have to travel would be greater, and there is the added problem of giving birth to a child with a larger head. To maintain the same performance would require more energy and our brains at the moment utilise about twenty percent. It's a matter of efficiency, and at the moment we are at the best balance between several parameters."

Demetrius nodded in agreement, "What you say is correct. What is needed is a better way to transmit those signals without increasing size or consuming too much energy."

"And you think that these new-born children have a different method of transmitting signals?" Elizabeth asked, and Demetrius nodded.

"Over time they will interbreed with normal people, and that is how the bug will infect a large number of people," Crooke said.

"Happy New Year folks!" Donovan raised his glass of water, "We live in interesting times!"

Demetrius raised his glass, "That is a Chinese saying that can be a blessing or a curse!"

Elizabeth felt that it was the latter and just sat staring at her plate.

"There are a few things that haven't been explained," Crooke held up his fingers, "One, who killed the drug baron? Two, where did the sand come from in that young officer's shoes?"

"This is where I get confused as well," Elizabeth agreed, "Ramirez was alone when he died, or so we think, so who pulled off his head and limbs? We looked very thoroughly for signs of someone or something else, and there is nothing other than Ramirez and why did he stop there? He could have run in any direction."

"I think I can answer the last question," Donovan held up a finger, "Your 'plane accident' was across his path and that would have meant masses of troops and police – if it had been real, so he went to ground."

Elizabeth gave a short laugh, "I'll have to remember that the next time we want to catch a fugitive! What about the dismemberment?"

"It may seem impossible, but perhaps he did it, Ramirez!" Crooke smiled at his companion's expressions, "The autopsy showed that he had taken a massive cocktail of drugs, and if we add our interstellar traveller, God knows what he would have been capable of!"

"But how did he pull off the last limb?" Donovan pointed out the obvious flaw in the theory.

Crooke leant on his elbows, "We have no idea what this bug did to him, and since he was already in a peculiar state, it could just be possible that two or more limbs were pulled off simultaneously."

"There is another scenario," Demetrius smiled apologetically, "He was firing at something, and we have assumed that it was a figment of his imagination. What if with the aid of the drugs and our bug the apparition became solid, and then vanished as his brain stopped functioning."

Elizabeth started laughing, "I can't put that in the report; they'll lock me up!"

"Demetrius may have something," Donovan pounded his head, "I can't remember the details, but something happened some time ago. It was if the person believed very strongly that the apparition was real, things could happen to that person's body as though they were attacked by a real, solid aggressor."

"I can't put that in the file either!" Elizabeth seemed amused.

"It's true; it has happened several times," Demetrius nodded, "Perhaps not as severely as this, but a person's mind can create powerful illusions. I suspect that something like that happened to Hamish."

"And the alien red sand, where did that come from?" Elizabeth asked, "We tested the sand and could not identify its origin; it certainly wasn't from the USA!"

Demetrius smiled, "Donovan has just suggested that the mind can perform some miraculous things, so perhaps the young man did actually travel to another planet and meet aliens!"

Elizabeth threw her hands in the air, "You mean that he used telekinesis, or was it 'Beam me up Scotty'?"

"I'm just suggesting a possibility," Demetrius reminded her, "I'll simply remind you that if you eliminate all possibilities, whatever remains, however improbable, is the truth."

"I read Sherlock Holmes as well!" Elizabeth snorted, "It is a basic truth in investigations, but I cannot accept that the mind can transport a person light years away."

Donovan ended the meal with an unsettling remark, "If what happened to Ramirez and the young officer were as we have suggested, that was the way it happened, then what else can happen?"

They left the Grill in a sombre mood and stepped into the cold air, Demetrius politely said goodnight, and followed Donovan to the latter's office. Crooke came last, tugging on his coat and stood next to the agent. Elizabeth shivered and drew the collar of her new winter coat tighter and looked up. The clouds had blown away, and the stars were crystal clear, hanging as they had done for aeons and making men wonder at the mysteries of the universe. As she looked, a shooting star streaked overhead, and she shivered again, but this time not from the cold, and she closed her eyes and made a fervent wish.

THE END

Printed in Great Britain
by Amazon

69720834R00180